Gnoll Tales

NightEyes DaySpring

Dancing Jackal Books

To Othello and the power of dreams.

Contents

Foreword

Anthropomorphic hyenas, or gnolls as they are often called, have been a staple of tabletop role-playing games (RPGs) for many, many years. Gnolls often get the short end of the stick, being nothing more than a type of monster to fight in the game with hunched backs and savage fangs. While gnolls increasingly are appearing in less monstrous roles in games and literature, they're still not getting the attention they deserve in order to be fleshed-out characters.

With the popularity of hyenas in the furry fandom, many furries know gnolls/hyenas make wonderful fursonas or playable characters in games. I had the chance during the COVID-19 pandemic to play a gnoll druid named Ingot Riverstone in an online D&D game, and it got me thinking about what gnolls who weren't regulated to being just monsters would be like. What would they feel, and how would they see the world covered in spotted fur, yet just as intelligent and wise as everyone else?

Ingot came from a game run by my friend Utunu full of magic, elves, dwarves, and of course, gnolls. He was always curious about history and the world around him. I started wondering what myths and legends someone like Ingot would know in a world of magic where his people are just one of many peoples in it. Because of these questions, and since there is very little published gnoll lore in fiction outside of them being savage, hungry beasts, I did what any writer does when they can't find the stories they want to read. I started writing my own.

Now, I'd like to share those tales with you and give you something to enjoy. The myths and stories here are tales gnolls might tell around a campfire to their adventuring friends or in a tavern over a mug of ale. So, sit down and listen as Ingot shares just some of the lore he has learned over the years with you.

NightEyes DaySpring, June 2023

Ingot's Note

Everyone has a story to share, if you ask them. Not all stories are long or complicated, but it's still their story to tell, and I've tried to listen as best I can. Even the trees and the rocks have stories, but it requires a special kind of magic to listen to those. As a druid, I've learned how to talk to the trees, so I've taken the time to ask them to tell me their stories. They're not the best conversationalists, but they speak of the wind, the rain, and the sun. Trees have simple concerns, and we should all wish to be as unhurried by life.

Now, you get far more diverse stories when you talk to dwarves, elves, humans, and gnolls. It's a big world out there, and everyone can tell you something if you take the time to listen to them. Unfortunately, gnoll folktales are not well recorded, so I've set out to change that. I've picked a few of the things I've heard over the years to get you started on your journey to knowing more about us.

Like any group, we're just as diverse as everyone else. Some of us or shorter or taller, and some of us even have striped instead of spotted fur. Some make great fighters, and others are excellent traders or crafters. And just like everyone else, we're complicated and layered, and that's wonderful, because if we weren't, we'd be just like trees. Also, trust me, after you talk to a few trees, you will appreciate these tales because these stories aren't just about wind and rain.

Ingot Riverstone

Stars and Moon

When the Old Gods created the world, they divided up the responsibilities among themselves. How exactly they divided the labor is unknown, but certain gods tackled certain problems together. From the songs of old, we know that the elf gods worked on the earth, sowing the bounty of the world we know now, while the dwarf gods piled up the stones that became the mountains. The human gods named all the things in the world, although the elf gods created their own names after hearing the names the human gods came up with. With how much the elves love poetry and song, we can only imagine they were displeased with the human gods' choices.

The gnoll gods of old, being strong and willing, chose to help out all over the creation of the world. They did not seek glory by making certain things, they sought glory by helping make everything better. Their paws were involved in shaping all sorts of different aspects of the world. They carved streams in the mountains the dwarf gods made, and fashioned flowers for some of the plants the elves grew. They created their own names and shared them, thus spawning another language when no one could agree on whose words for things were better. Yet one of the gnoll gods even undertook one of the most important tasks by herself. Aranya, the goddess of chance and fate, created the night sky. Without her, the night would not be as it is today.

There was a great discussion between all the gods before the work began. Once the gods decided to divide the night and the day, a lot of attention was given to the day. Time itself had been created by all the gods first, and the decision to divide the day was a major milestone in the process. The night was supposed to be a quiet period, so the task of making the night was not considered important. What to do with the night sky was left unresolved until the gnoll goddess Aranya volunteered to make it. She asked for only one thing to accomplish the work: a piece of the primordial fire.

Her brother, Oanyu, pushed for the other gods to allow her to take on this labor. Some though were displeased by her volunteering. Already, Aranya was well on her way to earning the reputation as the trickster we know her for now. She had been the one to push the gnoll gods to suggest their own names for things, knowing full well the elf and human gods were already locked in a struggle over words. Still, that wasn't why the elf gods did not like her request. They were concerned Aranya might attempt to give the primordial fire to the people who would populate this new world. They felt it was too dangerous for mortals to be trusted with such a powerful tool, but Aranya pointed out that magic, not fire, was the truly dangerous thing to give out.

This did not persuade anyone. The primordial fire was imbued with magic, and all the gods knew this. This fire is not the fire we know today but was a much more powerful thing that burned for as long as it was left to burn. It is what the sun is made from.

A great discussion was had, but Oanyu, who had already created the dawn and painted the colors we see as sunrise thought it fitting that his sister should make the night sky. He had carried primordial fire into the sky to teach it how to rise day after day and become the sun, so why shouldn't his sister have the honor of completing such a task?

No one disagreed that Aranya could have the honor of making the night sky. It was her choice in tools that concerned the other old gods. Yet Aranya would not be deterred, and she stood tall before the council of the Old Gods. To all those who disagreed with her, she asked how could she create the night sky without using something? They couldn't leave it blank, and she certainly couldn't take some of the earth and use that in the night sky. Since she spoke true, the other gods relented and gave her a piece of the fire. Then they left her to the task.

Her initial plan was to simply hang the fire a little further away than the sun and see how it looked. As Oanyu had carried the sun into the dawn, she could carry it into the night sky. Her sun was small and not a great burden to carry, but it still proved to be too bright. The ball of fire just made the night a softer day. Next, Aranya tried rolling out the fire into thin threads and weaving them across the sky, but after a few turns of the sky, the threads became bunched up and knotted. The work looked sloppy, and the other gods laughed at this. Aranya hung her head low and collected the threads, rolling them back into one single ball of fire.

Carefully and with great patience, she shaped the primordial fire into a sheet, making it so thin that it barely glowed. It took her days to knead and smooth out the fire, but that was nothing compared to the task of hanging it. This required an immense amount of work, and more than once the sheet fell to the earth and scorched it as layers of fire fabric pooled on the ground. Naturally, this caught the attention of the elf gods who were sowing the earth, and they came and scolded the gnoll god for her carelessness. When she pointed out she was working alone while they were working in a team, an argument that lasted four days broke out. In the meantime, the sheet of fire twisted and ripped apart as the sky turned.

When the dispute was settled and Aranya went to collect the primordial fire, she realized she'd burned some of the earth. The work of the elves in these areas was ruined, and this is how the deserts of our world were created. The elf gods of old never were able to make those lands fertile again, and even now they retain the heat of the primordial fire.

Frustrated with her failure, Aranya pulled down the fire she had already hung. She collected all of it back into a ball again. Then she climbed into the night sky to think. Her brother had painted the dawn and lifted the sun, yet she could not figure out what to do with the night sky. Frustrated and angry at her failure, Aranya seized the ball of primordial fire in her jaws and shook it. Sparks of fire shot out all over the night sky, but she cared not; her frustration knew no bounds. When she was done and tired, she had only a small bit of fire left. The rest had been scattered across the night sky. Sheepishly, she hung the now much smaller ball of fire in the night sky and crept back to her home to sulk and brood.

The sky turned, though, and the next night, when she went out to collect the fire she'd carelessly tossed about in her rage, she beheld her handiwork. Everything glittered and glowed in the dark, yet the light was just right, so any who sought to sleep could. The stars shone beautifully while the moon waxed and waned with the spirit of her determination. It had learned how to cycle its form from Aranya as she'd made and unmade the different night skies.

The task of creating the night sky was finished.

The One Who Tells the Story

I am not the only one of my people who is interested in our stories. When I was young, the small village I lived in had an old wise woman who was known only as the Claw Keeper. I'm sure she had a personal name, but I don't think anyone ever used it. She was a striped gnoll, with shaggy fur and blind in one eye. Her clothing was worn, and she wore only hides, not the fine linen of those who traded with the humans and elves.

The Claw Keeper lived by herself and prepared her own meals. However, in the warm months, when it was hot and we cooked outside, she would come sit by our fire and mutter to herself as she cooked her food. My parents treated her like she was a relative, but I thought her odd and kept away from her until one day she called for me to sit by her.

"Why do you not sit with me?" she asked, when it was just us by the fire.

Being only a few seasons old and having yet to learn the importance of tact, I was honest. "You talk to yourself."

She chuckled. "That's because I talk to the wind."

"Which is yourself."

She chuckled again and leaned forward so she could fix her good eye on me. "The wind will tell you much if you listen, Ingot."

"What can the wind tell me?" I asked.

"It can tell you where the birds go, and when rain will come. It can warn you of danger you are not prepared for, and for all this, it asks only for our words, which it carries away."

I tilted my head and looked at her.

"Perhaps when you're older you'll understand, or maybe you won't. Your fate is not yet determined."

My ears perked. "I have a fate?"

"We all have a fate, but what that is we may never know. Take you for instance. Your mother wanted a son, but you were small and weak when you were born. You weren't quite ready for life, so she named you Ingot to let life know it could temper you. It could keep working on you. Now you grow bigger and stronger. Is that not fate?"

I looked up at her, trying to figure out what she was asking me. The Claw Keeper's stripes were faded, and some of the adults of the village only tolerated her because she was an elder. One of the other cubs in the village said she lost vision in the eye when she sneezed too hard, and it fell out. She'd pushed it back in, but it never worked after. I was skeptical about that story though. I had sneezed hard already and still had both eyes. I realized I barely know her.

"I guess?" I offered. I didn't know what she expected me to say.

She laughed. "Ah, perhaps signs are not your strong point, or you wish to be modest."

"No, you say strange stuff," I replied.

"Oh, I do, but who doesn't? Now sit with me and listen, Ingot. What do you hear?"

Our village was little more than a cluster of small round-houses. There were a little over fifty of us here in the summer, although others would return to winter in the village after traveling to practice their various trades. Today was a spring day, and a fire had been built in the center to celebrate the completion of spring planting. Dusk was falling. It was quiet, save for the crackling flames and a few distant voices.

"Just the fire."

"And?" she asked me?

I tilted my head and swiveled my ears. "It sounds like some people are talking about hunting."

"Listen harder," she told me.

I did, and I could sort out the night insects awakening, and the wind, lazy right now, but still there. I told her so.

"What does the wind tell you?"

I tilted my head and looked at her in confusion, thinking she had gone daft. "The wind doesn't speak."

She smiled, amused. "Listen a little longer, young one, and focus on just the wind."

I rolled my eyes but did as she told me. The wind was just the wind, but on it there was a faint, wordless voice promising rain tonight. "It will rain?" I asked her, confused.

"Stay with the voice and listen to all it can tell you," she said, taking my small paws in her gnarled ones.

I did as she told me, and the voice promised a cold rain tonight and clouds quickly blowing by in the dark night. "I think it's saying it's going to be colder tomorrow."

The Claw Keeper took a sharp breath. "I see your fate now," she remarked, looking at me. "You have a gift. It will take time and work to master it, but it will serve you well."

"What if I don't want that fate?" I asked, concerned. Horrible things could happen to people, and what if one of those things was now fated to happened to me?

"Oh, you control it. I firmly believe that. Wait here," she said, letting go of my paws and getting up. "I will be just a moment."

She walked off, and I sat by the fire on my haunches, unsure what she wanted. I knew it probably was important I stay, but every part of my young body wanted to bolt and go play. I was restless and this exchange felt odd, but now that she had told me I could listen to the wind, I could do that if I focused on it. Did that mean I had crossed into adulthood? I barely had a mane yet, so I couldn't have, but why could I understand the wind? None of the other adults in my village spoke to it.

A few minutes later she returned carrying a small pouch. She reached into it and pulled out a leather necklace with a claw hanging off it. "I want you to have this."

Unsure, I took the necklace. "What does this have to do with the wind?"

"Nothing, but this claw belonged to a druid. She was a brave gnoll called Sniva, and if you can listen to the wind, you need guidance. I am too old to teach you much about the powers of nature, but her claw will give you strength. Few gnolls donate the claws from their paws when they die, but she did. It shall whisper to you what you can be."

I, being only a few summers old, had no idea what any of this meant. Obviously, my confusion was visible since she again took my paws. "It's okay, Ingot. She lived to a very old age before she gave up her claws. This is the last one I have to give during my journey, but I knew there was a reason I still had it. Her guidance is yours to listen to, and yours to ignore."

"But what does any of that mean?"

She smiled, showing her fangs. "You can be something special, but it takes work. There is the ability to touch magic within you, however it will take years of practice to master. For now, listen to the wind when you have time, and that is enough. When you're much older, it will be clearer. I will talk to your parents about this."

"Are they going to be mad at me for this?" I said, suddenly worried. They treated the Claw Keeper well, but even they thought her weird.

"No, no, no. I will take care of that. You do know what druids can do right?"

"They talk to animals and uh… hang out with trees?"

She laughed. "Let me tell you about Sniva. She's the one who taught me what I know, and from her story, you might see where you could go."

And that was when I learned something I could do that most people could not. I learned who the Claw Keeper really was and the journeys she'd undertaken in her many years. She taught me the first things I learned about magic, and the stories of our people that we don't always have time to tell. She showed me the life in all things, and while she was indeed old beyond years and could not teach me everything she knew, it benefited my understanding of the world greatly. When she died a few years later, I received her claws.

I gave half to the druid who finished training me, and I kept the others. I have given two to young gnolls who have shown great interest in my work as a druid and the history of our people. Each time, I tell them the Claw Keeper's story, and give them a claw so her wisdom can guide them. I hope to find suitable recipients for the others, and if I have an apprentice when I pass, I will gift them my claws, so they can pass on my wisdom.

As for Sniva's claw, I wore it proudly for many years until I had finished my training as a druid. Even today, I still carry it with me on my journeys, safe in the pouch the Claw Keeper gave me.

Stepping Through the Mists

Beyond the veil of this world lie others, and one of those is where the fey dwell. They rarely visit our world, but when they do, we must be careful. They are known to play tricks on the unwary, and some of the gifts they offer can be dangerous for those that accept them. One never knows what they might do, and because of this, gnolls have long been wary when fey are encountered. Sometimes though, one has to accept their help, even when they don't want to.

It is said the fey favor full moons to make the journey to our world, but they can choose to come anytime they wish. On the plains, where the grass is highest, gnolls sometimes become turned around and find themselves in places very different than where they just were. It was there, where the grass reached over his head, that a gnoll wandered into a stream that wasn't supposed to be there on a hot summer day. Favzu had gone to collect baobab fruit from a grove of trees that grew in a valley near his village, taking with him only his spear, his kukri, a waterskin, and a basket for the fruit, which he slung over his back. The journey was not long, and he had made the trip many times before, but this time he had somehow become lost when strange mists had overtaken the valley.

Confused by the stream, he stopped to get his bearings, and that's when he noticed the small elf-like creature the size of a young gnoll cub sitting on a rock near the water. It had wings like a butterfly's and spoke to him in a voice that sounded sweet like fresh honey.

"You look lost," said the fairy, "and you look hot."

It was indeed a hot day and his tongue had been lolling from his muzzle, but the gnoll was not foolish enough to let that catch him off guard. "I do not remember this stream being here," said Favzu.

The fairy smiled. "You may not, but it is here now," she said.

"Indeed it is," Favzu replied, looking back the way he had come, suddenly suspicious of the high grass. The mist had come in quickly, but it was strange to see mist on a day so hot. The sun should have burned it away by now.

"Perhaps you are confused. A cool drink from the stream might refresh you." She waved her hands and a glass chalice appeared, filled with water.

The sun was hot on his face, but he had heard never to eat or drink anything the fairies offered.

"Thank you, but I brought a waterskin with me filled from the well in my village."

The fairy dipped her wings. "Is our water not good enough for you?"

The gnoll knew that to refuse the gift a second time was dangerous, but it was also dangerous to accept it. In the stories he'd heard as a cub, eating or drinking in the realm of the fey gave them power over you, and could trap you in their world. What might seem like a day in the fey realm for him could be years in the real world.

"I imagine it is too good for me," offered the gnoll. "I am but a creature of rock and dirt, while you are a creature of air and light. I have never seen glasswork so finely done either. My paws are quite big as you can see."

"You may be a creature of rock and dirt, but neither of us are creatures of the water, and yet we both drink from the waters of the world just the same." The glass floated over to him. "Drink, and I will show you."

A third refusal was too much to make. With reservation he reached for the chalice and plucked it from the air. One moment it had been floating before him, and the next he could feel the weight of it as his digits closed around it. He knew if he let go of the glass, it would fall then, and the fairy would be angry with him. He lifted the goblet up and poured a little of the water into his muzzle.

It was light and sweet on his wide tongue, and he made sure not to let it run out of his mouth. It was like no water he had tasted before.

"The whole glass," said the fairy. "It will refresh you."

Favzu tilted the contents of the chalice into his muzzle. He did not spill a drop. In his stomach, he swore he could feel the water tickling at him as he lowered his broad head.

"There, that's better isn't it? You feel refreshed, don't you, and not so hot anymore I imagine?"

Indeed, he did not feel hot anymore. "You are right, I don't. Thank you. Where should I put your goblet?"

She made a flick of her hand and it was gently tugged out of his paw, and floated free of him. Then it disappeared. "Are you hungry?" she asked him.

He had eaten only some dried meat earlier, but he was hesitant to accept anything else from the fairy. "I would not wish to trouble you for food. I am off to collect baobab fruit."

"It is no trouble," she said, taking flight. "Wait just a moment." The fairy flew over to an orange tree nearby that Favzu wasn't sure had been there a moment ago. The gnoll shifted uncertainly, as the fairy flew up into the tree and plucked an orange from it.

It was obviously quite heavy for her for she struggled with it, but the fairy brought it over to him and dropped it into his open paw.

"Take this. When you get tired on your journey or thirsty, eat it."

The gnoll looked at the orange carefully. It was perfectly round and the rind was unblemished. "And if I'm not hungry?" he asked, looking up at the fairy.

"Oh, you will be."

Favzu tilted his head, confused. "I will be?"

"Oh yes," said the fairy. "Travelers like you always are. Consider it a parting gift for your journey." Then she lifted into the wind and flew away, leaving the gnoll alone by the stream that was not supposed to be there with an orange clutched in one paw and his spear in the other.

On the other side of the stream Favzu found a path he'd never seen before. It made sense since he had never seen the stream, but this one felt different. The trail looked both abandoned and yet well maintained, almost as if the grass had been sculpted to grow away from it. No strands bent over the path, which considering how tall this grass was, felt unsettling to him.

He debated for a few minutes before setting out on it. He did not know where it went, but he did not know where he was anymore either. In a situation like this, a path—any path—is better than just wandering around, and this trail had to go somewhere. Plus, the grass was much too tall for him to get his bearings. He could have climbed the orange tree, but he did not think that would lead him where he needed to be, and he wasn't sure he wanted to even attempt that.

He walked for an hour, the path weaved over gentle rises, but the scenery never changed. The grass was always taller than he was. Even if he jumped, he could not see over it. He thought the grass might go on forever when it suddenly ended at a line of thorny shrubs that reached well over his head and covered the path. The transition was so sudden he stopped to consider it carefully. He stood in the light of the sun filtering through the tall grass, but the path now continued into a dark and twisting maze of vines and branches that made the trail look like it dove into a great forest, yet no trees seemed to grow there.

"This makes no sense," said the gnoll out loud.

"That's because you are no longer in your world, my friend," said a voice all around him.

Favzu jumped and dropped the empty basket he had been carrying. It fell into the shade. He gripped his spear in both hands, ready to stab whoever or whatever might try to attack him.

In front of him sat a mouse, in the middle of the path through the woods. It tilted its head and looked at him before it scurried off into the dense underbrush.

"You can't fight me, gnoll," said the voice. "I am everywhere."

"If you're everywhere, why are you here talking to me?" he snapped.

The voice laughed. "That's because you have something I want."

"Which is?'

"The orange. Leave the orange on the trail and proceed."

He'd put the fruit in the small pouch he had at his waist, unsure of what to do with it. "The orange?"

"Yes, the orange she gave you. Leave it in the path and proceed without it."

Favzu looked back the way he came through the tall grass. "If you are everywhere, why not get one yourself?"

The voice grumbled. "Because that's the one she gave you. That's the one I want."

He hadn't wanted the orange, but he wasn't sure he wanted to give it up either to a voice that came from everywhere. "She said I would get hungry on my journey. What do you offer in trade?"

The voice was silent for few moments. "Give me the orange."

"No," said Favzu. "How do you know I even have the orange anyway?"

"You dare question my request? Fine, do not use my path then."

The tall bushes suddenly shifted and vines grew before his very eyes. The gnoll stepped back as the way before him vanished, leaving him on a path that led nowhere. Where once there was a passage, thorny shrubs now blocked his way. His basket was just inside the thorns now.

The gnoll stood in shock, unsure of what to do. The path led under the bushes, but there was no way he could cut through this. It would take hours to make a way with his small kukri, and if the voice could make the vines grow, it could likely do that again. He was stuck in the tall grasses that reached over his head. Confused, he turned around and followed the path back to the stream. He wasn't going to risk fighting the thorns to get his basket back.

❧

By the time he reached the stream again, he was hot and getting tired. His hunger had increased, and he was thirsty. He sat for a minute by the water on the rock the fairy had sat on, watching the ripples in the water. Finally he decided to dip his footpaws into the water and let it cool him. This was refreshing, and it made him feel relaxed.

Thirsty, but unsure whether to drink from the stream, he uncorked his waterskin, and went to tilt it back into his muzzle, but the skin, which this morning had been full of water, poured out only sand.

Startled, Favzu coughed and spit out grit as he dropped the waterskin. With apprehension, he picked it up and tilted it over the ground. Sand ran out of it until it was empty. He had no water, and had brought no food with him for what was supposed to be a quick journey. He had drunk the waters of the fey realm, and he was now trapped in their world. The only thing he had to nourish himself was the orange and the fruit still on the tree. He could drink from the stream, but the land he was in seemed featureless and vast. While the path had climbed small hills and descended them, it never gave him any vantage to gain his bearings.

With nothing else to do, he walked over to the tree and looked it over. The trunk was smooth and healthy. The branches were low enough he could reach them. He put down his spear and was about to start climbing when he heard the voice of the fairy from behind.

"I already gave you something to eat."

The gnoll froze and slowly turned around. "I'm lost," he said.

"Lost? You were just here."

"Yes, but where is here?"

She laughed. "By the stream of course."

"Yes, but where is my home? Where are the baobab trees?"

She flew over to him. "That is a much harder question to answer, and only you can answer it."

"I don't know where home is anymore. I followed the path and it took me to the thickets."

"No, no. That leads to the dark forest. You don't want to go there. Mortals who go there never return. Go the way you came on the other bank. It will take you home, but if you want to reach the baobab trees, you will need to continue through the grass on this bank."

He considered. He wasn't sure, but he thought the sun was already shifting to the west. "I will go home," he replied to the fairy.

"Very well, then cross the stream and you will reach home."

He picked up the spear and his empty water skin. He crossed the stream and glanced back at the fairy. She seemed amused, hovering there, but she made a shooing motion. "Go on."

With that Favzu plunged into the tall grass with no earthly idea where he was going. Behind him, he heard one last piece of advice from the fairy.

"Don't forget to eat."

შ

The gnoll walked for hours, pushing his way through the grass, but he saw no features in the endless blades. It never thinned and it never got low enough for him to catch his bearings. The only reason he knew night was falling was the light turned golden and began to fade. He was thirsty and hungry, but still he pressed on. When he had walked far longer than it had taken him to reach the stream originally, he stopped and tiredly sat down.

He was stuck in the fey realm. The village shaman had told a story a moon or two ago about the dangers of accepting gifts from fairies, but what choice did he have? The fairy has been insistent. Now he was trapped. He sat there in the fading light trying to figure out what to do when his stomach growled, reminding him he had not eaten anything in hours.

Tiredly he pulled out the orange from his pouch and considered it. The fruit was still the most perfect orange he had ever seen. With nothing else to do, he began to peel the fruit, digging his claws under the skin and removing the rind. When he was done, he carefully sniffed at it.

It smelled sweet, much sweeter than the bitter oranges they grew back in his village. He split it in half and pulled off a slice and popped it into his muzzle. The juice was flavorful on his tongue and the taste refreshing in his dry, parched muzzle. He was so hungry then that he quickly devoured the orange, leaving him only with the peel.

With the fruit now eaten, he looked at the peel, fingering it with his thick furred digits before dropping it onto the ground. He felt better at least, but he was still hopelessly lost in the grass.

The gnoll stood up, picked up his spear, and took stock of his situation. The sun was down now and soon it would be dark. Already the night insects were out singing in the tall grass. He sighed and closed his eyes and walked forward, feeling the grass and the gentle wind that ruffled the tops of the stalks.

He had only gone half a dozen steps when he felt cool mist on his face and ran smack into a thatched wall.

Startled, the gnoll fell back on his haunches, his eyes flying open. Before him was his hut. He was home! But how? Why?

He stared at the hut, confused. One of the other gnolls in his village, his friend Gnezoc, was walking past him and stopped.

"Are you okay, Favzu?"

"I'm… fine," he sputtered out.

Gnezoc gave him a curious expression, ears focused on his friend sitting on the ground. "Why are you just sitting here in the dark?"

"It has been a long day."

"Oh right, you went out to the baobab trees."

"Yes, but I uh… didn't make it. I got a bit lost for some reason."

"Lost? You?"

Favzu shrugged and got up. "Yes, I ended up somewhere else."

"Have you been drinking too much tej?" his friend asked with a smile.

"No! I just…" the gnoll paused, considering. "I was here and then I wasn't here. I was in a different place. I met a fairy there."

His friend stopped smiling. "You were in the fey realm?"

"Somehow, and then I was back here." He pinched the bridge of his muzzle. "I was lost, but she gave me this orange. After walking all day, I was tired, so I ate the orange. Then I closed my eyes for a moment, stepped forward," he said, mimicking for his friend, "and I was here," he added, stepping forward and splashing into a stream. Startled again, his eyes flew open.

"You really need to focus on where you want to be when you do that," said the fairy. "Also don't do that too much in one day. It will wear you out."

His heart was racing, pounding in his ears. He was back by the stream. "How am I… here?"

"You're still learning to control the power."

He turned around. His village was gone. "But I was just home."

"And now you're here," said the fairy, flying over to him. "Did you not know you could summon the mists between worlds before today?"

He stared at the fairy blankly.

"I assumed not, but you do it so easily, I thought I should ask to be certain."

"Did you do this to me?" he asked.

"No. A few in your world are born with this power. A small piece of the fey world attaches to them for some reason. All I did was help you unlock it by giving you a bit of this world so you could fix it in yourself. I understand the ability is mostly seen among the elves, but others sometimes manifest it too."

Favzu just stood there with his mouth hanging open, unsure of what to do.

"Might I suggest you first summon the mists with your eyes open, then step into them? Also, focus on where you want to be."

"I can do that?"

"Of course!" she laughed.

Favzu tilted his broad head, even more confused.

"Fine, a little instruction," she said. "You mortals don't understand these things without that it seems. Think of where you want to go, and see the border between the worlds. Then enter it and decide if you want to be here or in the other world."

He thought for a minute of his home, his village, and where that was. Slowly a mist formed, and he could see it in his mind. He took a deep breath and stepped in. The world suddenly changed and he ran smack into Gnezoc, who was frantically searching for him. Together they both fell onto the ground.

"Favzu, are you okay?" someone asked, pulling him off of Gnezoc, who was giving him a panicked look. "What is happening?"

"I am fine," the gnoll yawned, suddenly very tired. He shook himself to get his bearings. "Oh, that does take a lot out of you."

A crowd had formed outside of his hut. Everyone was shifting from foot to foot nervously, ears low, as the village shaman came up, carrying her staff. Rya looked at the crowd and frowned.

"Everyone give him some room." She knelt down next to Favzu and tilted her head. Carefully she examined him with an eye that saw more than just the normal world. They said she could see magic itself. He had not thought much of that, but now as she studied him, he could tell. She reached out and ran her digits over his body, tracing lines that were not there.

"What happened to you, Favzu?" Rya asked. She reached out, put a hand on his shoulder, and closed her eyes to mutter a few words. "You are different now."

"I somehow was in the fey realm."

"Ah, is that what I'm seeing? You've been changed. You are now more than you were."

"The fairy said I was born with this, but she helped me focus it. That I can summon the mist between worlds."

The shaman considered, crouching next to him deep in thought. It was Rya's job to protect their clan from forces that could threaten it beyond the ordinary, and others would have turned against Favzu. Some might have banished him from the village or had him killed right then, but she was not a foolish woman. She saw the chance to learn more and to pass that knowledge on. She took Favzu to her hut and had him repeat everything he had seen and wrote it down. Then after he rested, Rya took him out of town and had him demonstrate his powers.

It is from these two that we learned to understand the border between worlds and the magic that the lands contain. The gift to walk between realms is still far more common among elves than gnolls, but we learned much from it. From the teachings of Rya and Favzu, the first druid circle formed among the gnolls, and we came to understand more of the forces of magic. Even the wizards among our kind trace their earliest bits of arcane knowledge to this tradition.

As for Favzu himself, they say he never did grow old, but that one day he walked into the mist and never returned. It's possible he's still in the fey realm, still learning, unaware of how much time has passed in our world. Perhaps someday he will return.

The Dice Game of Stripes or Spots

When the world was very young Aranya carved the first dice from a piece of the bones of the world. Oanyu, who painted the colors of dawn and dusk had a bit of black left over and he added it to the sides of the dice to give them different meanings. He and Aranya enjoyed rolling these dice and guessing what the results of each die would be. From this, they devised the first gambling game, and taught it to the other gnoll gods, and then the gods of all the other peoples of the world.

Aranya had a reputation with dice, and it this is why the realm of chance and fate became hers to direct. If she wanted to, she could know the results of the dice before they were even rolled, but she found there was no fun in that. She liked to be surprised, and not knowing the result was the part that mattered most. Only when she wanted to impress the other old gods did she push and pull against the currents of fate.

Everything then was new, and the forms of the gods were ever changing. Since he had painted spots on the dice, Oanyu made his fur spotted. Aranya, who enjoyed the streaks of luck the dice could give chose stripes for her fur. The question though of what to make their people look like was one of hot debate among the gnoll gods. They had settled on the shape they wanted to give their children, but the patterns of their fur they could not decide.

"We should be one people, shaded like the earth," said Uratu, the goddess of the hunt. "It will give our children an advantage in their hunts."

"Perhaps so," responded Nin'nan, the protector god of clans, "but should they be striped or spotted?"

"Do we need markings?" asked Uratu.

"How would they know who each other were without their noses? The other gods are making their people all a little different," said Aranya. "Why shouldn't we follow their lead?"

"They could just paint on their markings," offered Svinya, goddess of war.

The oldest gnoll god, Hirash, the gnoll god of knowledge, then spoke up. Even then, when everything was new and still changing, he had seen much, for he had been first among the gnoll gods. It was he who had made the others, and they all respected his counsel.

"My children, you each have chosen to mark your fur differently, and it would be foolish to think our children wouldn't want to do the same. Perhaps we should use the dice Aranya has carved and ask them."

Aranya felt her hackles stand up. "Should such an important choice be left up to the eddies of fate?" asked Aranya.

"It is better that than endlessly arguing amongst ourselves. I want you to carve us a die of six sides and have Oanyu paint two faces with lines and two faces with spots. Leave one side blank, and on the final side, paint one spot and one stripe. I want neither of you to roll the die while you do this. Aranya, you will be blindfolded after you carve the die, and so you will not know which sides Oanyu has painted."

The gods grumbled at Hirash's choice in painting the dice, but each agreed to this. Uratu was the only one who favored not having markings, while the others were evenly split between stripes and spots. The task set, Aranya went to carve the die. As instructed, she did not roll it. She then gave it to Oanyu and was blindfolded. Oanyu carefully painted the markings on the die, and when he was done, he set it down on the blank side to dry.

The next day, the gnolls met to decide how to paint their children. The die was presented to Hirash, and he carefully inspected it. He smelt the stone to make sure it was true and wise. He tested it with his fangs to make sure it was solid, and when he was satisfied, he gave the dice to the blindfolded Aranya.

"Roll it. Whatever fate we see, we shall all abide by," he told her.

Everyone's ears perked forward, eyes locked on her paw, as she vigorously shook the die, and then threw it into the gathering of gnoll gods. They all refused to breathe as it sailed through the air and struck the earth. It bounced across the smooth stone ground of the meeting area and came to rest with the stripe and spot side showing.

"What is the result?" asked Aranya, for she could not see the result.

"It is the side with the stripe and the spot," said Oanyu, picking it up.

"Roll it again then," intoned Hirash.

Oanyu gave the die back to Aranya, and twice more she rolled the die, and each time it fell on the side with the stripe and the spot. After the third time, Hirash picked up the dice and threw it himself, and it again fell on the same side.

"It's weighted," accused Uratu, with a snarl.

"I cannot see what sides the symbols are painted on," said Aranya.

"There is no need to fight over this," interrupted Svinya. "War will come to the world later. Let us each roll and see what comes of it."

There was a murmur of ascent, and each of the assembled gnoll gods rolled the dice, and each came up with the same result, except for Oanyu, who rolled last and got a spotted side. There was much shock about that, but from this, Hirash understood the currents of fate. He decreed that most gnolls would be spotted, but that some would also be striped, for we as a people should not all be the same.

The Fox, the Wolf, and the Gnoll

We gnolls enjoy the simple life when we can. While some of us are magic users, warriors, or tradespeople, some of us aren't. Some of my clanmates are simple farmers just trying to get by. It can be a hard life, but that's fine. Up north, there's a gnoll named Alun who has a farmstead in a small valley. It's not a large holding, but he can grow enough crops to get by, and in the winter, he enjoys sitting by the hearth swapping stories with the local townspeople.

Now, if you're going to tell a good story in the middle of winter when the nights are long and the snow covers the ground you're going to want a good drink to go with it. Alun happens to also be a brewer, and he supplements his income by brewing beer and spirits for the local tavern. He makes good stuff too, because even the local dwarves appreciate his drink, and most dwarves have a very refined taste when it comes to drinking.

Even when you have everything you need, there're usually some things you want you just can't quite get your hands or paws on. It was on a snowy winter morning a few years ago that Alun went out to find some juniper berries. Alun wanted to make some spirits strong enough to blanch his spots and make even the hardest warrior feel its effects. He had some juniper trees by the side of his house, but it can take two to three years for the berries to ripen. The trees he had were just out of season and not ready to harvest from.

Without the fruit he needed on hand, he decided he was going to forage for some berries in the nearby forest. Alun's mate Shana had told him to bring back a deer or rabbit if he could, and she'd stew it with some of the berries. So, with a basket in one hand, and his bow slung over his shoulder, he trudged out into the snow. It was just past the winter solstice, and the snow was deep, the wind blowing bits of it around. Alun's fur had thickened for the winter, but he'd still slung a warm cloak over his tunic. There was no point freezing his tail off like a fool. He also packed a little dried meat to tide him over since he wasn't sure how long he'd be gone for, and it was better to have it and not need it than go hungry.

Setting off, his paws crunched through the snow as he walked across the farm and crossed into the woods. The stand at the edge of the field he'd already harvested earlier in the season, and while some ripe berries might be near the top of the trees, trying to find something left on them seemed like a fool's errand. He stood a good chance of falling, and that would likely leave him buried in snow if he fell, and who knows what he might twist or break. He didn't want to have to make Shana fetch the cleric while his three young cubs fretted about their dad, and he was pretty sure the cleric, an elf of so many years she'd lost count, would give him a tongue lashing. He could hear in his head her lecturing him about foolishly trying to pull fruit off a tree just to flavor some drink.

It was a good day to forage, although there was the hint of coming snow on the air. Alun admired the quiet of the woods as he hiked toward the nearby hillsides where he knew some juniper grew. He thought he'd spotted nearly ripe berries there a couple months ago when he'd gone out hunting, so hopefully they were ready by now.

The first stand of juniper he checked had already been harvested. Whoever had done it had only taken some of the berries, so it was probably one of the innkeeper's family. They always left some berries behind. He was able to pick a few there, carefully pulling them off the branches so as not to disturb the tree. It would be faster if he cut some branch tips off, but that only cut down the number of berries the tree would grow in the future, so he wasn't going to do that.

The gnoll then headed to the next group of trees he knew about. These had many more berries on them, and he was just starting to grab some, when he noticed a red fox sitting in the snow, looking at him.

"These aren't grapes you know," he said to the fox, which just flicked its ears, but didn't move.

Instead, it sat there, watching, waiting for something. Alun frowned and felt his ears lay back, but he ignored the creature and returned to collecting berries. He was almost done with one branch when he heard a crunch of snow and looked back at the fox. It had come closer and was looking at him intently.

"You're a brave little guy," he said to the fox, and after thinking for a moment, he tossed one of the berries into the snow in front of the fox. "There. Now let me get back to work." He turned back to the tree.

"All those berries, and you are only going to just give me one?"

He froze and looked back at the fox, and then glanced around. "Who said that?"

"Me," said the fox. "Who else are you going to talk to out here?"

Alun dropped the basket, and backed up, away from the fox. "You talk?" said the gnoll, startled.

"Yes," said the fox, walking up and putting their muzzle into the basket. "If you don't need all these, I'll just help myself."

"When did foxes start talking?" mumbled Alun.

"We didn't just start talking. Well, I did, but that's because of a druid, but anyway. Do you need all these?"

"Need what?"

"The berries!" exclaimed the fox. "I can't reach them, and you're so much better than me at picking them."

"I..." he trailed off.

The fox tilted his head and looked at the gnoll. "You?"

"You talk!"

"Yes," replied the fox. "Is a talking vixen a problem for you?"

"Foxes don't talk," stammered the gnoll.

"It's my understanding that hyenas don't talk either, but you talk."

Alun was taken back. "Yes, but I've always talked. Also, I'm a gnoll, not a hyena. Well not a four-legged hyena," he said, gesturing to his furred body and the fact he stood on two footpaws.

"Lucky you, I guess," she remarked. "I met a druid, and now I talk."

"There is a druid here, in Fairview Meadow?"

"There was, and uh, what's Fairview Meadow?"

"That's the town."

The fox scratched at an ear. "Oh, so that's what you people call where you live. Anyway, back to the berries, are you going to eat all these?"

Alun wasn't sure what to say, but what was he going to do, say no? "You can have some," he replied.

The fox dipped her muzzle into the basket and carefully nosed out some berries from the overturned basket. When she'd taken about two dozen, she started to munch on them.

"These are much stronger than blueberries," remarked the fox. "They're not as sweet."

"They're juniper berries," responded Alun.

"Ah… I learn something new every day." The fox paused. "You have a name also?"

"Yes, Alun. Do you?"

The fox sat back and considered for a moment. "She didn't give me a name, but I think so. I like the fall. Is autumn a good name? She told me the fallen leaves matched the color of my pelt. I wanted a pretty name."

"Yes, and who did this to you?"

The fox scratched behind an ear. "Who made you?"

"My parents."

"Oh, right, you talk naturally. Well, it was a woman who said I had a great destiny to fulfill. I think she wanted me to spy on some bandits, but that didn't work out, and she had to leave. I tried to follow her, but they chased her pretty far. Since then, I've been wandering around. Not many people to talk to who want to talk to me."

Alun knelt down and reached out a paw to Autumn. "I'm sorry."

"Thank you," said the fox, tentatively sniffing at the offered paw, before moving forward to try and get Alun to scratch her ears, which he did. "Ahh. Thank you for this. There's an itch I can't reach right between them."

"You're welcome," said the gnoll, picking up the basket with the other paw. He still didn't have enough juniper berries for what he what he wanted to do, and now he was going to need to harvest more.

After a minute the fox broke off, and went to sit a few feet away from him, so she could watch him. Alun, not sure what to do, stood up. "I guess I should continue my picking."

"I can come with you," offered Autumn. "I don't have anything to do, and the woods are dangerous."

He patted the bow, which still rested on his shoulder. "I'm no ranger, but I know a thing or two about how to shoot."

"Yes, but I'm kind of lonely," pleaded the fox, "and I would love to have someone to actually talk to. There's so much more I can say now that I couldn't before, and you know things I don't."

"Well, I guess for a bit," responded the gnoll.

"Thank you," said the fox, dipping her head.

Autumn watched as the gnoll circled the tree, picking the berries from the low branches, careful not to take the needles off. While these had more berries, he left some for the next forager. When he was done, he scattered a few of the berries so the tree could seed itself, something that confused Autumn at first.

"Leave those be," Alun said, pointing to the juniper berries he'd tossed away from the tree.

"Why throw them away?" she said, sniffing at a berry he'd tossed off.

"The trees need to grow just like we need to grow," remarked the gnoll. "It's something the druids teach."

She sat down and considered. "Is this a type of farming?"

"No, but you can't eat all your seeds, otherwise you won't have something to plant next year. That's just basic farming. Anyway, on to the next stand of juniper."

They set out further up the hillside. There was a breeze and slowly the sky was filling up with thick clouds, and the scent of snow on the air was growing stronger. Alun pulled his cloak tighter over his tunic but pushed on ahead. If he was alone, he might have turned back now, but he wasn't. He had Autumn with him, and if she could handle the snow, so could he, even if his pelt wasn't nearly as thick as hers.

As they continued up the slope, he stopped a few times just to check the sky and see how the weather was changing, and make sure his bearings were right. The snow was thick too, and he sunk down to his knees in a few places. Autumn stuck behind him, hopping from each of his larger pawprints to the next.

"That's a curious way to travel," he remarked when he looked back and stopped to watch her traverse the snow.

"Well, you have a curious way to travel in the snow. You don't break trail like a four-legged creature."

"My legs are a bit longer than yours," Alun said.

"Show off," said the fox.

The gnoll shrugged and continued up the slope through the trees. The final group of junipers he wanted to look at was next to a rocky outcropping, and from there he could look down into the valley and see the fields of both his farm and the neighbor's. At the far end of the valley, the houses of Fairview Meadow were clustered where the King's Highway ran through the valley.

And on top of the outcrop something stirred, and a head of gray fur popped up and stood up on long legs with paws built for the snow.

It was a wolf.

Autumn came up behind Alun and froze.

"Stick close to me and you'll be fine," advised Alun. "He'll move on."

The wolf's ears went back, and he dipped his head to stare at them.

"We should go," whispered the fox, turning around.

"Autumn…" growled the wolf. "Is this what I think it is?"

The fox froze in mid step. Slowly she turned back toward the wolf. "Hi Scruff."

"Here I let you go see who lives down there, while I rest my tired paws, and next thing you know you're making friends with people without me? I barely got a good nap in, and you've already abandoned me!"

Autumn laid her ears back. "You know I couldn't do that."

The wolf approached them, hackles raised. "No? Did she even mention she had a friend?"

"Uh no…" Alun responded.

The wolf growled low. "You can't just leave me out here! I can't just go back to the pack like this."

The fox huffed, annoyed. "Scruff, no one wants to adopt a wolf. You're not cute like I am."

The wolf stopped growling, and his ears drooped. His tail drooped behind him. "You don't know that. I'm cute, right?" he asked, turning to Alun.

Alun wasn't sure what to say. "You're more rugged than cute," said the gnoll.

"Rugged cute?" he whined, ears going back further, tail still.

"Yeah…"

He puffed up his fur. "See Autumn, he likes me."

"He just met you, and I hadn't even started the 'can we stay here' bit and now you've gone and ruined all the surprise."

"You left me!" huffed the wolf. "I'm not a yearling anymore. I belong in a pack."

The fox sighed and walked over to the wolf through the thick snow. "I know buddy, but can you at least let me try and find us a home?"

Alun cleared his throat. "It sounds like you have someone to talk to," remarked the gnoll.

Scruff gave the fox a glance. "You tried that again?"

The fox sighed. "What else can I say? Hey, let me hang out around here and catch mice? Who needs that?"

"That's actually rather useful for a farm," said Alun.

"Wait, it is?" turned the fox in surprise. "You need a mouser?"

"Two perhaps?" asked Scruff hopefully.

"Scruff, wolves aren't mousers."

"Are too! Although it's what you do when you're a lone wolf."

"He's not going to just have deer you can chase, Scruff."

"It's not my fault you can't keep up," huffed the wolf.

"I don't have the bite for deer!" she replied.

The gnoll cleared his throat. "Why did a druid awaken two animals?"

"There are things I couldn't do for her," said Scruff. "She needed a less noticeable scout, and while I can move silently through the brush, people tend to react violently when they see a wolf in the bushes. Autumn is smaller, and less likely to attract arrows."

"I'm the silent type," added the fox.

The wolf shook his fur out. "Right, well you tipped them off by trying to ask them for food."

"Would you leave that be? I told you I'm sorry. I told Brenna I'm sorry."

"Brenna is dead, Autumn."

The fox shrunk down. "I know… It's my fault, but I didn't know. I thought since I could talk to her, I could talk to them, and see what I could learn from them. How was I supposed to know they were going to come looking for her! And now she's gone, and here we are alone, and no one needs us now, and I can't get this stupid voice out of my head, and it's—"

"Shh…" whispered Scruff, as he came and licked the fox's face. "I'm here, and I'll help you figure it all out. It took me a while to understand what Brenna did to me, and to accept it. As long as we're together, we'll be okay. Being awakened isn't so bad, but you need to keep positive about it."

Autumn just sobbed. "I didn't ask for this! I didn't ask to be given all these words and not have the knowledge to understand what they all meant. Look at me, who needs a fox that talks? Who knows what to do with one of those!"

"I know," said Scruff. "I had more time to learn then you did."

The fox shrank back and shivered. "I want my old self back."

"You're still you," said the wolf. "You're just more than you."

Alun walked over and crouched down next to Autumn as Scruff moved to the side. "It's okay. Magic does weird stuff, and I don't understand it myself, but you're going to be okay."

She blinked her eyes and whined. "You're just being nice to me because I'm pathetic. Brenna awakened me because she needed someone to do stuff for—" She froze when Alun reached to scratch behind her ears. "I hate that this feels so good."

The gnoll chuckled and flicked his ears. "I've had people try and do that to me because they think it will soothe me, so I know it's condescending, but oh does it feel good. I have a farm, and you both can stay there. You just need to leave my sheep alone."

"Alone? They're easy hunting," exclaimed Scruff.

"Yeah, well they're my sheep, not yours. You'd be my guest."

"Oh, I'm a guest," said the wolf. "I get it. It's that social stuff you people do."

"What's a guest?" asked the fox.

"It's someone who comes to stay with you that you look after, but doesn't do anything useful," said the wolf. "They're like a pup, but they're often an adult. Brenna had a few guests at her hut when it was just us."

"Oh, well I don't know about the being useless bit."

"Well guests tell you stories, so we better think of some," said Scruff, "and not just ones about what you ate yesterday."

The gnoll considered. "I have cubs you can play with. They always need to be watched. You do like kids?" asked Alun.

"Pups?" asked Scruff.

"Kits?" asked Autumn.

"Children," responded the gnoll. "I have three of them, and a wife."

"Ah, that's what the other scents are," said Scruff, wagging his tail. "I'm great with pups. I regurgitated food for the ones my pack raised last spring."

The gnoll frowned. "That's not going to be necessary."

"I can't help nurse them, but I can sit with them," said Autumn. "I will teach them how to be quiet on their paws, and how to be swift like me."

"I can teach them how to howl like a wolf," added Scruff.

Alun sighed. "That's not necess—" he stopped himself, as both their ears went down. "You know what, maybe they can learn something from both of you."

Autumn started wagging her tail excitedly and Scruff gave a soft wag. "You sure?" asked the wolf. "I know we're a little different."

"It will be fine."

The wolf wagged his tail and came up to nose Alun, who reached down and rubbed behind his ears. Autumn bounded over and joined in excitedly.

"We found a home again!" she exclaimed excitedly.

"With food!" said the wolf.

"Well, I might need you to hunt for yourself," remarked Alun. "Everyone has to work on the farm."

"So, I can have one of the sheep?" asked the wolf, eyes big.

"No!"

He tilted his head and let his tongue roll out. "Fine, fine, I can go see what's in the woods. You know, if you stop picking juniper berries, I can flush out some deer for you to try and shoot with your bow. You do know how to use that, right?"

"Of course, and that would be useful," said the gnoll. "Shana, my wife, would like some game for dinner."

"Just give me a haunch and the rest is yours," said the wolf, bounding off into the woods and then pausing. "Hey Autumn?" he said.

"Yeah?"

"Thank you," he said, before he turned and trotted off.

"Do you think he can find a deer?" Alun asked.

"Oh yeah. He's a great hunter. It's a lot easier if you don't have to catch them and just drive them toward someone."

That afternoon Alun brought home fresh meat, juniper berries, one fox, and one wolf. Since then, his farm has run a lot smoother with no mouse problems and easy game in the winter. As for his beer and spirits, those have been selling well in the local village. Everything has been going well for him, except for the fact Scruff taught his children how to howl like a wolf.

Still, it's a good life, even if sometimes it sounds like a whole pack of wolves is living under his roof when Scruff gets the kids going, but that's exactly the type of life he wants to live.

An Accidental Apprentice

Curiosity can be a dangerous thing. There's a reason you don't randomly pick up unknown magical artifacts lying on the ground without first inspecting them carefully. You never know what something could do, and it takes skill to control magic. Druids and clerics find their magic by communing with nature and the gods. As a druid, I gain insight into what I can do by focusing on that connection.

Arcane magic is different and requires years of dedicated study to master. Wizards spend most of their lives buried in their books, honing their skills. Of course, there are a few people who just have an innate sense of magic that just comes to them, but even they benefit from practice and refinement. No matter how you do magic though, having something to focus your magic through like a wand or a staff gives you structure you can't achieve on your own.

Because of that, magic users guard their tools wisely, and those that go out seeking adventure often carry a second magical focus with them. Teenagers though, tend to just get into stuff, even when it's something they shouldn't touch, and that's exactly what happened when a gnoll named Gikx found a wand of polished wood lying under a tree just outside of his village. It was just sitting on a rock, as if it was waiting for someone.

Seventeen summers does not give you a lot of life experience, but he'd still seen wizards practicing. There were many wizards who liked to visit the nearby city of Breslax to perform tricks of light and magic in the sky for the Festival of Swirling Lights on the summer solstice. They would compete to have the most awe-inspiring illusions. Gikx's parents had been traveling the two hours journey every year since before he was born to see the lights, and he had dreamed of someday standing there with the wizards of the land casting great displays of magic and light into the night sky.

Of course, being from a small village meant that instead of being apprenticed to a local wizard, his parents had apprenticed him to a local blacksmith. The only fire he was going to get to control was the one in the forge.

Now, having found a wand, his heart raced. He'd dreamed about learning magic, but that had never been an option for him until now. His heart raced as he knelt down in front of it and tilted his head to inspect it. Could this really be magical? He put his forepaws on the ground and leaned down close so he could sniff at the wood.

The wood smelled like a combination of many things, and yet it didn't quite seem to settle on just one scent, as if it changed the longer you smelled it. It made the hairs on the tip if his muzzle stand up and it made the inside of his noise tickle, almost as if it made the air next to it cool and fizzy.

Gikx sat back on his haunches to consider what to do. He had planned to go swimming and meet his friends that day, and he had been on his way to join them when he noticed the wand. It was suspicious to find an item like this just lying by the side of the road, resting in the only shade among the fields, but who was he to judge? While his friends were expecting him, this find was something he couldn't pass up.

It was his path out of the forge, and into the life he had only been able to dream about. So, he picked up the wand.

The moment he did, his pelt felt like it was filled with magical energy, and the mane of fur on the back of his head and neck immediately stood up straighter. The enchanted wood was smooth and cool in his hand, unnaturally cool for a warm, late summer day. The two days a week he worked for the village smith were boring and entailed doing menial work around the forge. The three days a week he studied in school to finish up his education were little better. Gikx had already mastered almost everything they had to teach him. This though, was something new, something different. It offered all the promise of what he dreamed his life could be like, if he could just puzzle out its secrets.

The gnoll rubbed the pads of his paw over the shaft and felt the way his fur seemed to shift as if directed by an unseen force. He lifted the wand up and sniffed at it again. Again there was that strange fizzy sensation, but it was subtly different, as if it was filled with electric energy now. The smell also was everything and nothing at the same time. It was if there was earth, smoke, ice, and lighting all fighting to be smelt. Thae only thing it conclusively reminded him of was the night air during the Festival of Swirling Lights, as the wizards cast their smells.

Unsure what to do, he gripped the wand in one paw, twirled it for a moment, and then pointed it at the tree.

Ice shot out from the tip of wand and froze solid around the base of the tree in a spectacular display of magic. Shards of ice shot out all around, and some of the magic reflected off the tree and struck him since he was so close to the trunk.

Gikx's ears went straight back and his tail curled against himself protectively. He lowered the wand and looked at the tree and then back toward the wand. Then he checked himself. The black stripes in his white fur were frosted over, and he brushed snow and ice off his arms and clothing. However, the tree seemed to have taken the worst of the spell, since a couple of inches of ice now encased the base. He walked over to touch the ice with his other paw, feeling the coldness against his paw pad. The base of the tree was frozen solid.

Looking back at the wand, Gikx wasn't sure what to do. The ice on the tree would melt, wouldn't it? He didn't know, but if it melted before anyone noticed, he wouldn't have to worry about this. He could keep trying to learn the wand's secrets.

Except this wasn't his wand. It had obviously been someone's wand, and they had left it behind for some reason. Where they were though, he didn't know. Maybe he should talk to the village elders and see what they thought, but if he ever wanted to get to the festival as a wizard on his own, he couldn't give up this wand. This was his road to a better life, one where people wouldn't just see him as a smith or an iron-monger, but as someone really important.

He glanced around, suddenly unsure of what to do, but no one was there. The birds and cicadas were quiet, disturbed by the sound of magic. He waited a minute and they started to pick up their songs again.

Carefully he tucked the wand into his tunic and start-ed back to the village, hoping no one had seen the outburst of magic or would notice the ice. Anyway, it was a hot day, it would have to melt. He tried to remain calm, but his tail wagged. His mind was racing with possibilities. What else could the wand do? Did this mean he had the arcane aptitude to be a wizard or was this just something he could use to do tricks with?

He'd need to be careful as he figured out what it did. If he cast the wrong spell, someone could get hurt or killed. The last thing he'd want was to set the house on fire or freeze one of the neighbor's kids. It would take time for him to learn, but this was his ticket to the Festival of Swirling Lights. Or was it?

What if this wand only shot out ice? Could it do sparkles of light that didn't set things on fire?

He looked back at the tree. Its base was still frozen, but there was something else he hadn't noticed. A set of frozen paw prints led from it toward him. His footpaws were smoking from ice that encased them, and he realized suddenly how cold they were, because he couldn't feel his toes anymore.

Panicking, he pulled out the wand and tried to turn the spell off. "No, stop. You don't want to do this. I need you not to do this," he cried out.

Nothing happened.

In desperation, he pointed the wand at his footpaws and thought about warmth, trying to dispel the ice effect.

And that's when a fire exploded around him, catching the fence by the side of the road and alighting the crops in the field a blaze.

He blinked and dropped the wand as he took off running, the heat of the flames engulfing him.

Screaming, he ran from the fire, his paws sizzling in the blaze as magical fire and ice met and clashed. People came running to see the commotion, and the sight of a gnoll with his paws encased in ice and tail ablaze was the talk of the village for years after that.

It also attracted the wand's owner, a middle-aged human who had been a journeymen wizard for many years. He was able to quickly quench the blaze and dispel the effects on Gikx without anyone getting killed, although a few outbuildings were lost. Afterward, the two of them had a chat about magic, where he proceeded to lecture the gnoll about the dangers of just picking up random magical artifacts, no matter how benign they looked.

"I stopped to pull out my canteen, and I swore I had put it back in my pack," said the wizard.

Gikx looked down at the ground, ears back, tail between his legs. He'd been standing on his burned paws getting this lecture for the last ten minutes, and he just wanted to sit down. "I'm sorry, sir," he said.

The wizard sighed. "It is partially my fault, I admit. I should have been more careful. That wand has a way of getting lost, I've noticed. There's some spell on it that I haven't been able to figure out that seeks out people with the gift of arcane magic. I see it found you."

"Does that mean I have talent?" asked Gikx, his ears shooting up.

"You have the untrained ability of youth, and you're more a danger to yourself than anyone else. The wand let you focus that energy. However, if you'd accept training, I'd be happy to give it. It is time I took on an apprentice to pass on what I know. I don't tempt fate when it comes to leaving people with skill to their own devices."

The gnoll swallowed hard and nodded. "I would like that."

"Then let me speak to your parents, and I will see if I can arrange an apprenticeship. Just know it will be a much longer and more intense apprenticeship than the one you have now."

Gikx left the village a few days later to accompany the wizard back to Breslax. It was still a decade of hard work before he got to debut his skills at the Festival of Swirling Lights, but his parents were there to see, including most of his home village.

As for how he discovered his talents, Gikx has not been bashful about sharing the story. The illusion of a gnoll running across the night sky spitting fire and ice has become his signature element for the shows.

The Forgotten God

The gods who created the world ruled over it and us for millennia unknown, but there came a day where they all passed into the shining realm and ceased to be. It wasn't just the gods of one people who were suddenly gone either. All the gods left together to fight in the God War, and none of them survived. After that, the age of mortals came. We were forced to rule ourselves and have done so ever since. It has not been easy to get the bickering people of the world to agree, but without our gods, we had to find common ground with each other. It took generations for the laws we know today to be written, but slowly we the people of the world came to understand each other. As for the creator gods, they left us very little. Some of the relics of their power were fought over, but others were simply forgotten.

One of these lost relics was a temple deep in the misty foothills of the primordial forest. Centuries came and went, and it waited to be discovered. Few are sure why it went unnoticed for so long. It is possible wards were placed over it to keep out intruders and these had to wear down over time until they would release the temple back into the world, but it is also possible it was just too remote for someone to find it. Even today, parts of the primordial forest are still full of uncontrollable magic we know little about, and those areas are best left to do their own thing. There are simply areas human hunters did not venture into and even the elves are hesitant to tread. Yet even with a wilderness full of dangerous magic, eventually someone will come along willing to explore it.

A young gnoll is the one who finally chose to walk into the shrouded mists, and set out to map the rivers and streams that reached into the foothills. Thyrm was a druid, and it was the sworn duty of his order to protect nature. To do that though, they needed someone to explore the area and map it. They considered sending many people to do that task, but they did not know what lay in the forest. They settled on sending one person to carefully explore, and he would report back what he encountered. They could have sent a man or an elf, but they sent a gnoll. We are fortunate that they did. I would not be able to tell you some of these stories if Thyrm had not undertaken this task.

The forest was thick and hard to penetrate. The trees blocked out the sun, while thick vines and mists made travel difficult. Even for someone so skilled as a woodsman, it was challenging for him to keep his bearings. Sometimes the mists would play tricks on the gnoll and he would walk in circles for hours. Often Thyrm had to use his magic to fly up above the trees as a raven to reorient himself with the lay of the land. He was trying to find the source of a stream deep in the foothills when he encountered the temple. He had been following up the stream's bank, making mental notes, when moss-covered glyphs on a rock by the water's edge caught his attention. They were well worn, suggesting they had been there a very long time, and that immediately piqued his curiosity; he'd seen no signs of civilization for days. He inspected the markings carefully and then searched nearby to see if there were others.

At first, the gnoll wasn't sure what he'd found, but the massive stone slab he encountered half-buried in the ground had to have been erected by someone. When he found three more in quick succession, he began to suspect this had once been a grand complex. There was quite a bit of cut stone poking out of the ground, but all of it lay hidden under the ancient trees that grew here. He'd overflown the forest multiple times and never noticed this place.

Thyrm tried to trace the layout of the complex, but much of it was buried, lost to time. There appeared to be several ruined structures here, yet only the bones of stone remained. Ruined walls were scattered in the woods along with stone columns reaching up to support roofs that had long since fallen. He suspected many buildings had included extensive wooden parts which had long ago rotted away. There were reliefs, but almost all were broken or worn. The stone surfaces in many places were too damaged to tell what they depicted. There was also something about this place that made him clutch his staff tighter, made him pause to listen carefully to the sounds of the woods. When he found a courtyard cut into a hill, he knew what about this ruin was sending shivers down his spine and into his tail.

A statue of a gnoll stood in the middle, its features weathered, but still visible. Nearby, an intact wall contained writing carved in the common alphabet. These were the same letters he used to write in, but the words were all different. He reasoned this was in the old tongue, the one the common trade language had developed from. There was one word though carved in the stone that stood out, and his heart sank realizing its meaning had not changed over time: 'god.'

The context was lost to Thyrm, the meaning of the inscription impossible for him to understand, but this single word told him much. This was once a sacred place, but it was also a secret place. The storytellers spoke of the traditions the people of the world once followed that were now lost. None of the gods had survived the coming of the false gods and the God War. The names of the gods were no longer spoken because those names had no power anymore. The elves and dwarves still sang of their lost gods, but the gnolls did not. For this place to have been a temple to a gnoll god, it had to be thousands of years old.

It appeared it had lain here undisturbed for generations, but he couldn't be the first to find it, could he? When he'd prepared for this journey, he'd found nothing in the old records about there being a temple in the forest. He'd encountered no name or reference to a lost temple, and yet a place this big must have once been incredibly important. Perhaps it had always been hidden, and this was why the forest around it was so impenetrable.

He looked around, trying to ascertain if there was a danger he should be aware of, but the only sounds he heard were the sounds of the deep woods. The birds seemed unconcerned about his presence. The only scents his nose picked up were of leaves and moss, yet there was a feeling of there being more—something just beyond his senses that was more like an itch than a scent or a sound. He leaned forward to sniff at the rocks, but all he could smell from them was wet stone.

The gnoll considered, looking at the inscription and the courtyard cut into the hill. Should he be here? Maybe not. Maybe he should leave because there was a reason this place sat undisturbed, but Thyrm also wanted to know why it was here. So much was forgotten and lost, and so little known about the passing of the gods, that this discovery could be an invaluable source of information about the God War. He needed to document the find and bring that knowledge to his order. They would take this to the sages who would be able to decipher the inscriptions. The druid had not brought tools to survey the ruins with, so he would have to do his best. It would be difficult for him to return and guide anyone else here, so it was important to get as much information as he could now.

Thyrm found a reasonably dry spot in the courtyard to sit and make some observations. He carefully made notes about the statue. He copied down the inscriptions to show to his order. He counted off how many paces the courtyard was to get dimensions. While he was doing this, he found his next major discovery at the side of the courtyard cut deepest into the hill. Behind thick vines, half-buried by dirt, there was an opening with a passage into the hillside.

He finished his notes about the courtyard and then studied the portal he'd found. The passage smelt strongly of earth, and while dirt had built up over time, he was able to push his way in. While the entranceway was tight due to the obstructions, once he was inside he realized he'd found a grand arcade cut into the hill. This too had been decorated with detailed carvings, although in the gloom of the stone tunnel, it was difficult to tell what they depicted. There were also more inscriptions, but he didn't see any that used the word 'god.'

The gnoll could see well in the dark, but the entranceway was the only source of light. The further in he went, the harder it would be for him to find his way. He crouched down to scent the ground, and that's when he caught it, very faintly mixed in with the smell of earth and stone: the scent of another gnoll.

He sniffed around, trying to see how long ago they'd passed this way, but he couldn't tell. He'd not noticed the scents of any others in the courtyard. Maybe there was another entrance to this underground area. Also, if someone was down here, would they want company? They could be using the complex as a hideout, but who would be hiding this deep in the woods? Unless he'd gotten turned around, the nearest village was a two-day hike through dense forest.

He frowned. The scent was very faint. Maybe it was old, something the stones had held onto from another wanderer.

There was only one way to know, he told himself, as he stood up and took a deep breath. He whispered the incantation and the tip of his staff lit up with a soft light. With that, he started down the passageway.

It was cut straight into the hillside and seemed to be level. After a hundred or so feet, two chambers opened off the corridor. The one on the left appeared to have been a storeroom of some kind with decayed baskets stacked against the wall. Mostly it was dirt with bits of weaving still present. Whatever had once been in there had long since rotted away. Thyrm idly poked at the remains, and they broke apart in his paws.

The chamber on the right contained the remains of some type of statue that had been smashed when part of the ceiling had come down. Stone and pottery fragments lay scattered on the floor. The walls were unadorned, and the purpose of this room escaped Thyrm. It could have been a shrine or a place offerings were prepared. The gnoll took a cursory look around, but nothing caught his attention. The remains of the pottery would be of interest to the sages, so he left the shards undisturbed,

Another hundred feet down, the passageway opened up to a pillared chamber with a high ceiling, and it was here that Thyrm found his next major discovery. To the right of the entranceway, set into the walls, there was a grand wooden door, and next to it hung a single torch, flickering in the still air.

The gnoll carefully crept forward and examined the torch. At first, he worried it was a sign of recent activity, but it gave off no heat and was some type of magical effect. How long had it been here? Its feeble light barely illuminated the room, yet it marked this entranceway for some reason. Perhaps it was the last bit of magic still here, hanging on in the gloom.

He took a deep sniff, and again caught the smell of gnoll. It was stronger here, almost as if the source was on the other side of the door. Thyrm studied the wood. It was carved with depictions of gnolls. The door was also firmly shut, the hinges rusty, yet still holding firm. They had not been opened in a long time, but if they weren't opened, how did someone get to the other side?

He frowned and debated with himself in the flickering torchlight before he reached up and grasped the iron door handle. The door loomed over him silently. He took a deep breath, tightened his paws around the handle, and pulled on the door.

The hinges at first didn't want to budge, but he kept tugging, and slowly they opened with a loud squealing sound. Anyone on the other side heard him as if he screamed his name, but that was not the biggest shock. Beyond the door, there was faint daylight, and that was because the chamber opened to the sky. An ancient tree grew in the middle of the opening, marking this as a sacred grove.

He stepped into the room and looked around the large circular space, and that's when he saw him.

A gnoll much bigger than Thyrm was kneeling before the tree. At first, Thyrm thought he might be dead, but the gnoll slowly turned to look at him and then stood up.

He was taller than Thyrm, taller than any gnoll he'd ever seen before, and clad in a simple tunic, and a pair of trousers that ended at the knee.

"Finally, someone has come," he said in a raspy voice with an accent unlike any he'd heard before. "I had thought I was forgotten."

Thyrm looked at the stranger as he approached and towered over him. "I wasn't sure if anyone was down here," he replied.

"Did my kin send you?" asked the other gnoll.

"I do not know your kin."

The gnoll tilted his head and took a deep sniff. "You are mortal," said the large gnoll.

Thyrm felt himself go stiff. "Yes… you're not?"

The large gnoll shook his head. "I am Oanyu."

"Thyrm."

Oanyu looked at him carefully. "You don't know who I am?"

Thyrm shook his head.

The large gnoll's shoulders sagged. "I should have known. I have wondered why they left me, but now I know. How did you find me?"

"I scented you in the passageway."

Oanyu looked at the open door. "And what magic did you use to break the seal?"

"I just pulled it open."

Oanyu's ears stood up. "None of the magic was left? How long has it been?"

"There is a magical torch outside, but it has faded."

"How long have I been here?" repeated Oanyu.

Thyrm chose his words carefully. "I don't know. The temple complex is in ruins. The God War was so long ago, I'm not sure even the sages know exactly when it happened. A lot was lost then. You really don't know how long you've been here for?"

The large gnoll shook his head and turned away from Thyrm. He started walking toward the tree and Thyrm followed him, unsure of what to do. "No, not anymore. I tried to keep time, but there was a point time stopped having a meaning and I just waited. I see now that my wait has been in vain. The secrets I have protected mean nothing, for there is no one to speak them to." Oanyu put his hand on the trunk of the tree and bowed his head.

Thyrm waited, but the god did not speak again. He just stood there, letting the silence drag on. "Should I leave you be?" asked Thyrm finally. He wasn't sure if he'd just been dismissed or not.

Oanyu looked up. "No… I am not used to company. I forget you mortals have such short lives. Tell me, what stories do your people sing of my kin?"

"We do not sing of the gods anymore. We haven't for a long time."

Oanyu wiped his face with a broad paw, and Thyrm could see the fur on the back of his hand was wet. "I should not be surprised, but are we all forgotten?"

"The elves and dwarves still sing about their lost gods, but we gnolls do not. The sages keep records, but the stories are not read by many."

"Did none come back from the shining realm?"

He took a deep breath. "The stories say they went to fight. They say a few came back, but the power of the survivors faded quickly, and they went to the afterlife. All the gods are now dead, and we have been left on our own."

Oanyu looked at the tree and then back to the door. "I can feel the truth in your words. I am the last then." He traced a paw along the bark of the tree, considering. "You wield magic, don't you? I can smell it on you."

"I do."

"Are there many mortals who can control magic now?"

"It's not common, but great mages and druids walk the land now."

"Then it makes sense why they left me."

Thyrm was curious. "What do you mean?"

"I am the god of the dawn and beginnings. When the world was young, I gave the sun the power to rise. I am the guardian of springs and sacred groves. I planted the sacred trees that formed the basis of the first temples, and I nourished them with my tears. I helped bring magic into the world, and without me, those seeds would have faded before they were strong enough to grow for themselves. Before the war, my fellow gods held onto magic for it was precious to them. Without them, it has flowed to the people, and with that the responsibility for the world."

Thyrm had spent enough time tending the trees in the sacred groves to understand the truth in Oanyu's words. As an acolyte, he had spent time maintaining his order's shrine. "Then what does that leave you?"

The god sighed. "I'm not sure there is anything left for me to do. The world continues without my kin and the other gods." He wiped his eyes again, and his voice cracked as he continued. "The world has grown up, and my time has passed. It was said the gods would eventually fade away, that the people would eventually be strong enough to stand together on their own, but not all wanted to see that. The God War may have been the way of bringing that about. My sister Aranya always was a sneaky one. She controlled the forces of chance and fate. She knew things the rest of us didn't. This may have been the best course she could see. I just wish I had been wise enough to say goodbye before they all left."

Thyrm could see the god was upset, and he could think of nothing to say, so he did what he did to anyone who needed comfort. He tried to hug Oanyu, even though he couldn't get his arms around him.

It was comical seeing the gnoll hugging the god around his navel, but the god only stiffened at first before he sagged. "Thank you, my child," said Oanyu, tears dripping down his face. "It has been a long vigil held in vain."

All Thyrm could do was hold the god and let him cry, and cry Oanyu did as the smaller gnoll held him. The god cried for almost an hour, big tears for the lost gods. When he was done, he was barely taller than Thyrm. The smaller gnoll was so wet from the god's tears, he had to shake out his pelt as if he'd gone swimming.

The druid brought the god out of the forest and took him to his order. They quickly realized Oanyu had given the last of his powers to weep for his lost friends. There was no more godstuff left in him. The great reserves of magic he once had were gone, his immortality lost.

A mere mortal now, there was little he could teach the sages about magic they did not already know, but he had detailed knowledge about the history of the Old Gods. The sages diligently recorded his stories, and from it the true scope of the God War finally became known. Oanyu's stories are how the Old Gods can again be remembered. It was also a new beginning for the world, one that was not at first obvious to anyone, including Oanyu.

While he only lived another forty years and died a mortal, Oanyu was well-loved by those who knew him. Thyrm came to spend quite a bit of time with him and came to treasure the mortal god's company deeply. There was also something about his great cry that awoke something Oanyu did not realize he could do. The river of emotion he gave that day, and the loss of his powers, gave birth to a new generation of gods who arose just before he died. They thanked their creator profusely, and still sing of him even today. They were different from the Old Gods because they did not come to rule over the world, but to watch and nurture it. The old gods had hoarded their powers, and in the end, fate had taken it away from them so that new, more benevolent gods could come.

The Death Dancers

In the mountains lies a volcano that towers over the nearby peaks we gnolls call Nur-Ba'Nkekur, which translates to the Mountain of the Hidden Fire. My people know that the fire inside slumbers even though the volcano is quiet and shows no signs of life, and we tell this story so we do not forget that fact. Nur-Ba'Nkekur may be dormant now, but it has woken up before.

There used to be a village of men who lived at the bottom of Nur-Ba'Nkekur next to a lake of pure water. The volcano's rich soil provided for the people, and the lake's fish were bountiful. The people of this village used to worship the mountain, but as time went on, they forgot about the mountain's fire. It had not erupted in so long, many thought it dead, but the elves who lived on the other side of the mountain were not so fooled.

Elves live longer than men, and their collective memory is even longer. Over the years, they noticed the subtle changes in the mountain, and kept notes. When the first wisps of smoke were seen escaping from the rocks near the summit far above the tree line, they consulted their histories and made plans. They grew saplings from the trees living on the mountain's slopes and the forest that surrounded it, then carried them away. They took their books and transported them over the ridges to a distant sacred grove. Finally, they decided to warn the people of the village of men about the danger from the mountain.

The villagers did not believe the elves. They said the elves were scared of the past. The mountain was dead, they claimed, so the villagers would not leave. The elves did not argue. They did not know when Nur-Ba'Nkekur would wake again, but they are a people who dwell on this earth far longer than the rest of us. They do not take chances with their lives. As a final concession to fate, the elves suggested the villagers talk to the dwarves, for they are born to hew stone. Dwarves can read a mountain better than anyone, and the elves will never dispute this. After that, the elves left their treetop homes in the lush forest at the foot of the mountain, and they did not come back.

Yet the people in the village did not seek advice from the dwarves. Instead, they went about their lives normally. The mountain lay quiet, and the villagers told themselves the elves were foolish. Instead of leaving, they celebrated their good fortune of no longer having to share hunting grounds with the elves or worry about their concerns for the forest. The people in the village danced long into the night to celebrate becoming masters of all the land around Nur-Ba'Nkekur. Then, seizing on the opportunity, they began to expand their village, turning it into a true town by welcoming outsiders and inviting them to settle.

Thrucot, a gnoll, was one of those people who moved into this growing town. He hailed from the foothills of the mountains, and he was a trader. The people in the town had many interesting things to sell him, some made by the people in the village while others were taken from the abandoned elven homes. He wasn't well liked by the townsfolk at first—

humans are often nervous when a gnoll moves into their town—but Thrucot had coin to buy with and goods to sell. With time, they saw him less as a mountain of fur and fang, but as a keen-eared trader with a nose for a deal. The gnoll built a home for himself and his son on the edge of town. He was already getting long in the fang when he moved to the village, but his son, Razux, was still young and not yet an adult.

Razux did not have the appreciation for trade and coin like his father did, but he did have an appreciation for the woods around the mountain for they were rich with game, and the beauty of the land compelled him to explore. The young gnoll took to spending his time hunting and communing with nature. Through many hours of study and listening to the advice from an elder in the village who knew the elves before they left, he learned to harness the power of the land. He listened to the voices of the trees, and through careful study of the animals that inhabited the woods, he learned how to take on their forms. Razux would sometimes spend weeks out in the woods before he'd return to town, and as part of his explorations, he climbed all over Nur-Ba'Nkekur to learn its secrets.

Eventually he found the steam at the top of the mountain and the bare spots it left in the snow. This baffled the gnoll at first, but as his magical abilities increased, he started to probe the stone, trying to understand what was happening. Razux was no dwarf, but reaching out with his senses, he could feel the heat of the fire inside of the mountain, and each time he tried to understand it, the hotter it seemed to be. Confused, he stopped trying to read the stone, and he asked the people in the town about the mountain and its past. The elves had been gone for a few years at this point, but the villagers were happy to tell him that the elves had been afraid of the dead mountain. Concerned that Nur-Ba'Nkekur was starting to wake up, Razux left the village to find a dwarf who could come and see the mountain.

Thrucot saw his son off, wishing him a swift journey and advising him not to dawdle. He suggested he go north, for the dwarves had a hold there and Thrucot had met traders from it before. Alone, but with a sense of purpose, Razux searched for where the traders his father had met came from. Yet finding a dwarf, any dwarf, proved difficult for him. It took him weeks before he could find the dwarves' secret underground hold cut into the mountains. More frustrating was the response he got from the dwarves when he did find them. They called his mission a fool's errand and said there no way to calm the fire inside Nur-Ba'Nkekur. It would do what it wished, and if the fire was so close to the surface that he could feel it with his magic, the volcano was close to erupting. Dwarves have an innate way with stone and if they don't think it can be salvaged, they do not waste their time trying to work it. The mountain of the hidden fire burned from the inside, and soon it would spill forth that fire from its peak.

Alarmed, the gnoll put his abilities to use and took the form of a wolf, running back to the village as quick as he could. Paws that were his, but not his, connected with the ground in a rhythm far different than how he walked. Before he'd held the forms of the animals only briefly, but Razux could not delay. He needed to return immediately and bring the warning the dwarves had given him. The gnoll-wolf ran for three days straight through valleys between the mountains, only to collapse on top of a ridge overlooking his home, too exhausted to keep the form any longer.

Razux had only been gone for one turning of the moon, but when he finally caught his breath and could find the energy to stand up to look upon his home, he was taken aback by what he saw. The mountain had changed in the time he was gone. A strange bulge had appeared near the summit that hadn't been there before, and a wispy cloud clung to the top of the mountain that seemed to be coming from the mountain itself, like steam rising from a kettle about to boil. Even though he was exhausted, Razux pushed on to town to make sure everyone was gone and help anyone left leave, but what he saw when he reached the settlement shocked him.

The people in the town were still there! But they were not making any effort to leave. Instead they were celebrating, preparing to hold a festival that very night with feasting and dancing. Confused, he sought out those whom he knew. They said the gods had gifted them a spring of hot water near the town, and the elders had ordered a special holiday in honor of the find. It was hoped that this special spring might be a gift to bring the town even greater prosperity. Razux was dumbfounded. Had they not noticed the strange clouds or seen the way the mountain was changing? He asked them, but while these things had been noticed, no one seemed to care. Nur-Ba'Nkekur was a dead mountain they told him, and it was not ever going to wake again. When he tried to let the townsfolk know what the dwarves had said, they walked away from him. Today was a day of celebration, they told Razux, and they didn't have time for foolish rumors.

Confused and frustrated by their lack of concern, the gnoll walked back to his father's house. There he found Thrucot waiting for him, a few things packed up and rations for the journey already ready to go. Razux didn't even need to tell his father what the dwarves had told him, for Thrucot could see himself that it was time to leave. He had waited for his son only because he hoped the news Razux would bring would convince the people of the town to leave with them. Saddened to hear how they disregarded the advice of the dwarves and continued to ignore clear signs of danger, Thrucot said that there was nothing they could do for the townspeople. They could only save themselves.

The two gnolls left that afternoon, taking only what they could carry, leaving behind many valuable trade goods. That night, when the people of the town were celebrating the gift they said their gods had given them, as they danced under the stars, Nur-Ba'Nkekur erupted, spilling hot ash and lava down its side. Some may have kept dancing until they were engulfed in the inferno, too foolish to even run. Even then it wouldn't have mattered since the mountain's fury came at them with a speed that no beast alive could meet. None of the townsfolk survived.

Today, no one lives in the immediate shadow of Nur-Ba'Nkekur. The town was destroyed completely, buried under suffocating ash and lava. Even the lake next to the town was wiped off the map. The gnolls who have told this story before me have not bothered to record the name of the town for it no longer exists. The elves still know the name, but no one has bothered to ask them. We do though have a name for the people who once inhabited that place. We call them the Death Dancers.

The Gnawer of Bones

Many wonder why my people keep old bones around in winter and do not bury them immediately. Well, I'll tell you. One winter the snows came down from the mountains to the grasslands so strong with snow so deep that even we gnolls could not travel between our villages. The nomads among my people were forced to shelter in place, wherever the storms caught them. It's not that we are unfamiliar with snow, gnolls live in the mountains after all, but the snows swept across the plains stronger and deeper than anyone could recall. And after the snow fell, the wind came, a wind so cold that our fur could not keep us warm. This wind tried to gnaw directly at our bones.

Many of the nomads perished, unprepared for such a strong storm. Theirs was a life on the move, and if they could not move, they could not live. The people in the villages fared better at first, but slowly the wind ate at them. Teeth marks started to appear on their houses, giant scratches etched by the wind. The wind was hungry, and it wanted to keep eating and eat it did. It stripped the skins off our tents, ate the wood off our homes, and when it finally broke in, it ate us, leaving behind only the bones of its victims.

No one knew what they could do. We started calling the wind the Gnawer of Bones for it would chew on the bones of those it killed. We had no idea how to stop a wind like this, but a young shaman came up with a way to save us. She saw that the wind left bitemarks on the bones it left behind because it was still hungry, so she decided to give it something to chew on. She took a shovel and went to the village's refuse pit with the wind following her tail. Slowly she started to clear away the snow and dig into the frozen ground, searching the decayed garbage. The wind bit at her, ripping at her clothes, and slashed at her, but she kept digging, desperately trying to turn up the frozen soil even as the wind tried to devour her.

It was coming for her throat when her shovel struck the old bones of a roast cooked that autumn and flung it in the air. The wind saw what she was offering and seized it, carrying the leg bone of the roast away. Frantically, she started flinging more bits of bone that had been buried in the refuse pile into the air. The wind kept eating, chewing on all the bones she gave it, howling for more. The shaman kept digging until she collapsed from exhaustion.

In the morning, the sun came out and people of her village emerged, amazed. The Gnawer of Bones was gone, but where was their shaman? They searched for her, and they found her naked but alive, still clutching the shovel in her paws. They carried her back to her hut, confused at what she had done. None had been with her for she had refused to tell anyone her plan for fear of leading them to their deaths. Only when she had recovered could she speak of what had happened. Since then, each clan has kept the old bones of their meals from when the first frost is felt until the spring thaw, for we never know when the Gnawer of Bones will return.

And those that don't? It's usually not a problem, but sometimes, when the winter is harsh, they go missing, their huts and tents torn apart by the wind.

The Gods in Between

In the drylands, trees are scarce because rain is infrequent. The hearty acacias that grow in these lands live short lives, but there is one that is so old it has seen empires come and go. This sacred acacia, which is infused by magical powers, is known as the Lover's Tree.

Many, many years ago, back when the new gods were first coming into the world, it stood alone, and it was just a tree. Then one day a gnoll named Renu came and sat under the tree to enjoy its shade and waited.

They were a curious gnoll, not because they were particularly special, but because they were always in between male and female. We do not know if they were born in between or just felt in between, but they were just in between. It matters not how they were born anyway.

Under the acacia Renu sat and rested. The tree offered good shade, and they had come to think. Some people told the gnoll they should craft like a male, skilled with their paws and keen with their eyes, while others said that they should hunt like a female, swift with their footpaws and strong with their spear throws. The village elders told Renu to just pick a path, but everyone wanted them to be something they weren't. Renu would have none of it. They were not one thing, but two things, and whomever they would love would need to understand that. On the advice of a village elder, it was suggested they go find a tree to sit under and figure it out.

The elder might have meant this as finding any tree and just settle the confusion with themself, but Renu saw this as a quest. Thus, they journeyed for many days, seeking the right tree, seeking the right place to think, and when they found that tree, they sat in its beautiful shade and thought.

The first day, nothing new came to them, and the next, nothing new came to them, but Renu kept thinking about who they were and what they were. Nothing changed, and confused on the purpose of the elder's advice, they stayed under the acacia. A passing shepherd, a dark-skinned human, saw them there and offered them water and Renu accepted it gratefully. Then another shepherd offered them some meat, and they accepted it too. Through all this, Renu stayed under the tree, and days turned into weeks. The locals assumed they were a holy person of some kind on a vigil, and they brought food and water to Renu who kept their vigil, deep in meditation.

After forty days, another gnoll came to the tree and sat with Renu. They too had always struggled to find who they were, caught between the genders, and together the two sat and meditated for a few hours, unsure of the other's plight until the second gnoll finally asked.

"Why do you sit under this tree?"

"I sit because one of my village elders told me I should sit under a tree and think through myself to find who I am," replied Renu.

"And are you that hard to find?" asked the other gnoll.

"I know who I am, but no one else knows who I am. They insist on labeling me one sex or the other, but I am both, and neither."

"Ah, I know that feeling," said the second gnoll.

"You do?" replied Renu, ears up in surprise.

"Oh yes. My parents wanted a boy, but I came out different. Neither one nor the other really."

"There are others like me?" replied Renu, hackles up in excitement.

"Well, there is at least me, but I have heard of others. We're not too common."

"Still, you see it, and you understand."

The second gnoll bobbed their head and nodded, tall wagging. "Yes. My name is Shena."

"Renu," they responded, getting up. "My vigil has been answered. If you would like, I can take you to my village and show the elder I am not the only one."

Shena considered. "Does the approval of an elder matter that much? If they could not see the you you always were, could they see the me I have always been?"

"No, probably not," said Renu. "Let's just talk, here in the shade. The locals have given me a bit of water and some dried meat, and I can share it with you."

"I'd like that," said Shena.

Renu and Shena stayed under the tree for two more days, talking and laughing. Then, coming to a decision, they left the shade of the acacia and built a hut next to it, and decided to live together there. Soon others came, and a small village formed around the tree, and each night, Renu and Shena would sit under the tree for an hour after dinner before bed. The gnolls and humans of their new village listened to them, and learned much about who they were and what the world was. They offered advice only on love and always gently, like a gnoll treats their newborn cubs.

Here, in this village, Renu and Shena grew old, and it was here they died, together. The people buried them under their acacia, careful to nestle them between its roots while not disturbing the tree. Then they told the story of Renu and Shena to the people of the nearby villages, and others came to the tree to sit and think. Not all were confused on who they were, but some were just lonely. Many a couple met under the tree.

A year passed, and under the tree on clear nights people started saying they saw things. There would be two gnolls holding hands, talking to themselves. And that wasn't the only curious thing about the acacia. People started feeling presences of great power when they saw these spirits and a sense of love and connection to each other.

The tree had born two new gods right here in their village, and since then, lovers of all species, dwarf, elf, human, and gnoll pray to Renu and Shena, the gods of love and patience. Together, they rule with the other gods, and their tree continues to grow and flourish, even though it has long outlived any other acacia in the world.

And on clear nights, sometimes you will find their spirits still, under the acacia talking together.

A Wager in Bone

The village of Two Taverns sits on a riverbank where the King's Highway crosses a large stone bridge. As the name implies, it does indeed have two taverns. One is a large luxurious affair that caters to richer travelers. The food is good, the rooms are clean, but you pay an extra silver or two for your room. The other, The Black Tod, has seen its cycle of good years and bad years. I got fleas from the bed there once and trust me when I say that was not a lot of fun. So naturally, I went back, since being a young, itinerant druid does not pay. This was when I was still just getting my paws in the mud back then, and I thought I could handle myself in a game of dice. Turns out I couldn't.

The Black Tod back then was best described as the type of place you only visit if you're desperate or broke, and I was a bit of both at the time. The owner at the time, Sammis, was an old human who should have retired and sold the place a decade prior, but he wasn't one to give up on a dream, and he knew the Black Tod could be something more than it was. The bones were good he would say, but the rest of the place needed work.

His apprentice was a dwarf by the name of Halvar Iron-spike, and he had already seen a lot by the time he came to the Black Tod, washing up with a group of mercenaries who were down on their luck and looking to drink the last of their coin away. Halvar and his friend Khalid stayed, while the rest of the party left town broker and more desperate than they had arrived.

Khalid was a dark-skinned man from far to the south across the vast deserts and savannah, and I've never figured out why he settled in Two Taverns, but he said he was tired, and he says it was as good a place to stop from the journey as any other. Halvar stayed because he drank more than he could afford to pay, and there was little point going on when you couldn't even afford a cheap beer. He chose to work off his debts, figuring it would be a short break from the road. Khalid had kept a few coins to himself, and he set up a little stall in the market working tin and copper, which quickly grew into a very profitable enterprise.

Thus I, being still green behind my ears with a spring in my tail, was an easy mark for these two to strip of every coin I had, which Halvar proceeded to do in a game of passage I should have bowed out of after the first round of beer. I stupidly stayed put, losing everything.

"Looks like you'll be sleeping in the stable at this point," said the dwarf, picking up the last of my coppers from the table. He smiled at me, pleased with his success.

"Eh, I've slept in worse places," I said dejectedly, picking up my mug. I'd lost count how many rounds we'd had at this point, but I could certainly feel it.

He shifted the coins in his hand, feeling their heft. "You want them back?"

"You giving me my money back?"

"One more wager," said the dwarf.

"I've got nothing left to bet." That wasn't true, but the things on me like the necklace the Claw Keeper gave me were not on the table.

"Oh, you've got plenty left to bet," said Halvar.

"Leave the gnoll alone, friend," said Khalid. "You've already put him outdoors."

The dwarf chuckled. "He ain't broke though. One of those gold earrings would fetch a good price."

"I'm not betting those," I responded with a snarl.

"Perhaps something else," said the elf who rounded out our gaming table tonight. She was a tall fair skinned elf called Alwine with delicate features, long hair, and a passion for dice. She'd asked to join our game when the dice first hit the table. She'd also had good luck tonight, but not as good as Halvar had. "You all seem the adventuring type."

"Former," said Halvar.

"Same," remarked Khalid.

"I travel and practice my craft, but it's small stuff," I responded.

"Ah, but you have your own staff. You are already a journeyman in the druidic arts, aren't you? I recognize the claw around your neck as a gift to guide you."

"I heal sick farm animals, and deal with the conflicts that farmers have with their cattle and any predators in the woods," I responded. "I know better than to get into old ruins where wild magic may run deep."

She smiled, and it was most unsettling in the way she leaned over the table to whisper at us all. "A staff is a powerful tool in the hands of one who can summon magic." Alwine reached under her cloak and slowly pulled out a small bone dagger inscribed with arcane sigils. "Perhaps we up the ante and all bet something we value."

There was silence at the table for a moment before Khalid spoke up. "I came for a friendly game, not to shake my life up."

"Wise, but what about you, Ingot?" she asked me.

"There is a big difference between losing money, and losing my staff," I responded. "Plus, a staff is useless in the hands of someone who cannot wield magic."

"May I?" asked Halvar, reaching for the dagger and then pausing.

"Yes, of course."

He picked it up and looked it over carefully. "Even I know this is worth far more than Ingot's staff. Why would you offer this?"

She smiled. "Perhaps a little chaos in all this."

The dwarf flipped the dagger over. "Is it magical?"

"Not to me, but maybe to him," she said, pointing at me.

I squinted at the symbols, and the way they were scratched into the blade. They had a familiar look to them. "That's gnoll made," I said.

"Perceptive. Do you know who made it?"

I motioned for Halvar to hand it to me, and I looked over the blade carefully. "It's inscribed in the old language, but the meaning is clear. It's a ritual knife for the gnoll goddess of dreams, Shamana."

"Indeed, she who guides the sleeping."

"Where did you get this from?" I asked, eyes narrowing.

"Oh, I won it in a game of cards a while back, but where they got it from, I can't say."

I carefully examined the curve of the dagger. The edge was not sharp, but it was finally cut and etched. "This would have been made from a hunter's kill, to guide them in their future. Probably for someone who had a small shrine to Shamana in their house. These aren't used in temples, but more for personal affirmations."

"So you know how to use it?" she asked me.

"I know a few ceremonies, but the new gods do not interfere in our lives. Devotion to Shamana is a personal matter."

"Well, will you play for it?" she asked me.

"I would not win," I said.

"What makes you say that?"

"I have not won at all, but perhaps Halvar will play in my stead?"

"I don't want that," said the dwarf.

"I know, but I will wager my staff, and you will roll the dice and make the calls."

The dwarf squinted at me and then at Alwine. "If she would let me."

"I will not play Halvar for your staff. Only you," she said.

"And I would not win," I responded.

"What makes you so sure?"

I cleared my throat and leaned forward, letting my muzzle drop. "Because I think both of you are cheating."

Halvar slammed his fist down. "How dare you! I would never cheat at dice. It's against my honor."

Khalid, who had been sitting out of this, laughed. "You are perceptive, Ingot, but you missed the biggest clue. Only Alwine is cheating. I recognize that tattoo on your wrist," he said to the elf. "It is a luck mark. It's small, subtle, and lets you influence the dice."

"You cheater!" snarled Halvar, slamming his fists on the table again. "I should have you thrown out."

She smiled and sat back. "Not many people know what those are, but I assure you, I did not cheat tonight."

"Luck marks are an old trick," said Khalid, "but they're not the only one. I've been to a lot of taverns over the years. Perhaps we should redivide the pot."

The dwarf glowered, but with the sizeable winnings he had, he said nothing.

"There's only so far you can go with a luck mark. It does not always work in your favor. So, perhaps a different game for the dagger," the elf said.

I glanced at Khalid. "How powerful is a luck mark?"

"It depends on the mark. May I see your wrist," he asked Alwine.

She hesitated for a moment and then reached over. He ran his fingers over the mark and closed his eyes for a moment as he muttered a few words. I could feel him doing something magical. "There is no luck left in this," he said when he was done.

"I know. It earned me a few coins over the year, but the magic has faded. I have not chosen to recharge it."

I picked up my tankard and took a gulp. "Well, I am still in the stables."

"Then let me sweeten the deal. The dagger and ten copper against your staff."

I put the tankard down and looked at the elf. She had some trick in this, and I would be out a staff if I lost this. It would take me a week to carve a new one, and that's assuming I could easily find the right wood for it. There was everything for me to lose, and I couldn't be sure my judgement was good anymore at this point.

"Fine, a final round, but not with these dice. We will play an ancient gnoll game and throw moons and stars."

"I do not have the dice for that," she said, but I was already in my pack and pulled out a small cloth bag. Gently I set it down and dumped out the contents of the bag. Seventy small wooden tokens each etched with a star along with two bone dice fell out, and her eyes lit up.

"Do you know the rules?" I asked.

Alwine reached forward and picked up the dice, looking at them. "Yes, but it rare to find sets of this. It retells the gnoll myth for the creation of the night sky, does it not?"

"In a fashion, yes. It's an old game. Not many play it anymore." I responded.

The elf chuckled. "I've heard the tale. Would you wager this against the dagger?"

I hesitated. "This is a family heirloom. It belonged to my grandfather."

"The better to bet then for a sacred dagger, don't you think?"

The human and the dwarf were looking at us. Halvar spoke up. "You seem insistent on besting him," he said to the elf. "Why is that?"

"I don't like to lose, and I follow the whims of the elven goddess of luck. Gambling to Damistariqel is a form of worship. To bet cautiously is to not believe in her powers."

"I'm not sure the gods pay attention to games of chance," said Khalid.

I considered for a moment. "I will wager the dice set for the dagger."

"Very well," said Alwine. "Halvar and Khalid shall witness this game, and the goddess of luck will bless us with her virtue. Shall the best player win."

I spread out the tokens and set the dice apart. "The first to twenty stars wins. Do you wish to go first?"

She picked up the dice and threw, the roll giving her a waxing crescent, and earning her one star. I picked up the dice, and threw them, earning myself a waning gibbous moon, losing two stars I didn't yet have. With that the game was off.

Luck was, like the rest of the night, not on my side. Alwine rolled well, and I only hung in there by rolling some waxing gibbous moons that let me steal a star from her. As the game proceeded, my paws grew sweatier as she stayed in the lead, her luck better. She quickly reached nineteen stars, while I was behind her at seventeen. It looked like she was going to get the dice set from me.

"This could be it," she said, picking up the dice.

"I know," I said dejectedly.

She threw the dice, and I watched them bounce across the table, feeling a sinking feeling. The waxing symbol came up on one, but moon die was blank. She'd rolled a new moon and lost her turn.

"Perhaps next turn," she remarked handing the dice over.

Nervously I picked them up and threw them, and the fates smiled upon me. I had rolled a full moon, earning one star from the pot, and one star from an opponent of my choice. This being a two-player game, I got one from Alwine, bringing me to nineteen and her eighteen, with me finally taking the lead.

The elf smiled and scooped up the dice and eagerly threw them, landing a waxing gibbous, thus earning two stars. My ears fall back. I'd lost the dice set.

"Good game," I whispered.

"One more wager," she said reaching over to my pot. "I'll only do a steal of one, and let you throw again, if you throw in one of your gold earrings."

"You're not required to steal on a waxing gibbous. You can take two from the pot or one from another player."

She smiled. "I know, but you've already lost your dice if you don't take the wager. They're a family heirloom, aren't they? Just like the earring is."

Our drinking compatriots looked at each other. "She's got you in a bind, Ingot," remarked Khalid. "You might want to back out now."

"And where's the fun there?" said Alwine. "When does a gambler quit?"

"When there's nothing left to give," I said.

She pulled out two gold coins from her purse and put them on the table. "What if there's more to earn? I'll give you another throw to see how this goes. I could even lose a star on my next turn, you know."

"I can't," I said.

"You can," said the elf.

"You shouldn't," said the dwarf.

"I wouldn't," said the human.

But you will, said a voice in the distance. My ears swiveled, and I thought I saw the figure of a tall elven woman in a long gown with a golden coin twirling in her long fingers, standing across the bar watching me.

"Ingot?" asked Alwine.

I turned back to her and then quickly glanced back to the bar. "I thought…"

Alwine looked at the bar. "She favors you it seems," she said, surprised, and sat back. "Take the roll."

"I…"

"Just take the roll."

I glanced back at the bar and back at the dice. Tail down and ears back, I picked them up and threw them. They sailed across the table and landed on a waxing gibbous.

"Ah," remarked Alwine. "It has been a good game." She pushed the dagger and the two gold coins on the table toward me. "Good game," she said offering me a hand.

I shook it nervously. "To you as well."

Then Alwine got up and walked away from the table, leaving me dumbfounded.

"What did you see, lad," asked Halvar after a minute.

"There was an elven woman by the bar, holding a gold coin, turning it over in her fingers. She said I would take the roll, but she wasn't there when I looked back."

The dwarf sucked in his breath. "The new gods do not interfere directly with the world. For you to see one must mean you have some destiny in your life to fulfill."

Khalid rolled his eyes. "Now come on, you can't be sure it was a goddess."

"It was Damistariqel," said Halvar. "Even Alwine knew it."

I didn't know what to say, so I picked up the dagger, and examined it again. "Maybe the goddess wanted me to have this? Although why an elven goddess would want me to have a dagger for worshipping a gnoll goddess, that I don't understand."

"Maybe," said Halvar. "It's hard to know what any of the gods want, if they want anything from us at all."

I shook my head and started to pack up the dice and tokens.

"So another round of dice," asked Halvar. "You've got money again."

"I'm going to quit while I am ahead. I'm not a devotee of Damistariqel."

"Not yet," said the dwarf with a chuckle. "Again, who knows where fate takes you, right Khalid?"

"Indeed," said the man, lifting his tankard. "Halvar, get us a round with your winnings and let's tell him about some of our time on the road together."

"If you want to tell stories, you can pay for the round," remarked the dwarf.

"I'd just get the money from your purse, my sweet."

"That man owns his own shop, makes good coin, and he won't even pay for his drinks out of his own purse…" the dwarf grumbled as he got up and went to the bar.

Khalid shook his head and turned back to me to whisper. "A word of advice, if you want to dice with Halvar again, bring your own dice."

"Wait, he was cheating?" I said surprised.

"In a fashion. He has a technique for throwing those that improves his odds, and he's been practicing with that set for a long time. The fates aren't the only ones who don't play fair."

"Uh, thanks," was all I could muster, "but why tell me? He's obviously your friend."

Khalid smiled. "Oh, he is and more, but if one of the gods is favoring you, I'd rather be on your good side. Plus, we really do need more people in this world doing work like you do. You deserve a good night's rest instead of sleeping in the stable."

Twisted Vows

"Your teeth are weak," is the first thing Kyla Tangledmane had told the young human noble when she'd met him at a court function. Kane had given her some vapid compliment about her traditional hip wrap, probably something his parents had told him to say, and instead of leaning on the etiquette her mother was trying to instill in her, she'd gone for the simple bluntness of her father.

Even though Kyla was taller than him, both were fifteen and just getting into court life. Kane Ellsworth blinked at her, surprised by the reply, before he responded. "And? You shed on the furniture, but you don't see me commenting on it."

The gnoll had smiled then, showing off her fangs. This human amused her. "Fair enough. If you don't mention my shedding, I won't mention your teeth," she replied.

"It's a deal," he said, and after that they'd talked with an ease that felt far more natural than two young nobles just meeting should have with each other. There was a kinship found due to the pressures their parents put on them, and the next time they met, a few months later, they once again quickly found themselves enjoying each other's company.

Seven years later, their wedding was set for the second full moon of spring, and a pact between their families was signed. As the second son of Lord Layton Ellsworth, Kane's marriage had not been of much importance, and he had been left to carry on with Kyla on his own terms. However, the death of his brother in battle the year before had complicated the family's inheritance and standing.

Kane's brother had already fathered four children, and if Kane took the dukedom and had his own children, it would mean none of his brother's children could sit on the thrown. The fact Kane was already involved in a noble from the city of Breslax was convenient and shored up his family's fortunes. The arrangement served both families well, especially since a human and a gnoll couldn't have kids of their own.

Outsiders might have thought it would be a loveless marriage, except it was everything the couple wanted. Lady Canice Tangledmane was all too happy to let Kyla have the husband she wanted. Kyla had grown to be a head and a half taller than Kane, yet sometimes she felt small in court functions. Even though she towered over Kane, Lord Ellsworth was too blind to see the way his son blushed when he looked up at Kyla. Instead, he saw her as a way to secure his legacy. By marrying her, Kane wouldn't mess up the inheritance and create a family branch that could lead to conflict, and this made Lord Ellsworth very happy.

Doing his part, Kane had spoken the words and proposed, and Kyla had given a restrained yes. She would have preferred to be the one to propose, in the traditional gnoll way, but she accepted the need to mollify the Ellsworths' pride. The arrangements were taken away from the couple. As befitting their noble rank, the families and the courtiers got to squabble over the how and why. Canice herself drove a hard bargain and while she couldn't set all the terms, she picked the date and the time, satisfying the desire to hold the ceremony under Aranya's creation of the night sky and the favorable fate this would give the couple.

"The blessings of the gods will carry you forward," she told her daughter after the arrangements had been set. "Tholla, steward of the night, mistress of the dawn, and creator of new beginnings, will smile upon you. Spring is her season, and the date is when her power will be at its greatest. The wedding will be in a grove sacred to Hannaril, the elven god of forests, and you shall drink the beer brewed by worshipers of Pivin, the human patron of merchants."

Kyla would have preferred to have an old seer throw some bones, mumble some words, and ask for the gods' blessing, but Canice Tangledmane was not going to let her daughter's wedding be wrong, and certainly not to a human boy barely her equal. His teeth could not crush bone like theirs. How could he hope to be a good husband to her without the gods' favor is he couldn't suck the marrow out of his kills to keep up his strength?

Kyla wanted to protest to her mother, but a marriage of political convenience, no matter how desirable to the people getting married, doesn't let you voice your own concerns. She had accepted the human way of doing things and let Kane propose. She had accepted her mother's spiritual concerns and the need to make sure the signs were right. Kyla even accepted the inane prattle of Kane's father, but there was one thing she just couldn't accept: the wedding dress.

"I am not wearing that awful thing. The dark red fabric clashes with my pelt, and something with that much volume has no practical purpose after the wedding," she had declared to her mother when the tailor brought the dress for her to try on. She'd not paid close attention when he'd measured her for it, but now that she saw it, she couldn't fathom wearing something with long sleeves that had fabric trailing off them.

"If the lady would try it on," remarked the elven tailor, "she would see it fits her well. I still have to add the lace."

"It has lace?" she said, alarmed. "Do I look like I wear lace?"

The elf looked at the elder Lady Tangledmane for guidance. She was dressed in a blue hip wrap and matching tunic, both embroidered with yellow thread, but it didn't restrict her motion like the wedding dress would Kyla.

"The design is a traditional human dress," remarked Canice. "It's been sized to fit you."

"That doesn't stop it from being ugly and impractical."

"Dark red is a traditional color for humans on their wedding days," responded the tailor. "It symbolizes the transition into marriage."

Kyla growled. "Do I look human to you?" she said, snarling at the tailor.

"I only made what I was asked to sew," he snapped back, unphased by her anger and sneer. "Your mother specified this."

"I had to give them something for the time and place," said Canice. "They requested a dress aligned with their family lineage."

"I've tried to make the tail slot in the back adjustable so you can control how it lays against you, and still have a full range of movement."

The bride grumbled. "The only thing worse I can think of would be a completely white dress that shows any stray fur."

"Kyla, I paid for this dress," said Lady Tangledmane, "the least you can do is make sure that it fits."

Properly chastised by her mother, she went and tried the dress on. Stepping back out, she felt like a ball of fur stuffed into a bag. She was used to wearing simple dresses when the occasion called for it, but this was far too extravagant for her. And the fabric high up on her neck made her pelt itch.

"Can't we just hire a wizard to magic a dress on me for the ceremony and I can wear something comfortable?" she protested to her mother and the tailor.

"Absolutely not," scowled the elf, checking how the dress lay on her. "You'll be in the middle of dancing and something will go wrong with the illusion spell. Then everyone will know you're wearing an illusion."

Kyla's ears went back. "I have to dance in this?"

"No," said her mother with a sad sound in her voice. "You have to waltz, and you have to do it eloquently."

꿈

The Tangledmane family was a proud clan, full of fighters and leaders. Lord Hevin Tangledmane was a gnoll of few words, and a known brawler back in the day. He'd have settled all his disputes through feats of strength, but that could only get you so far when someone could knock you out with a magical block of ice to the head. He'd learned that one the hard way and while he'd had to moderate his stance once he'd inherited his father's title, he still pined for the carousing of his youth with his brother and sister. Thus, he listened to his daughter's complaints patiently over a tankard of mead before he responded.

"Your mother handled the negotiation," he told Kyla when she was done.

"They've taken almost all the decisions away from me, including what I wear. Can't you do something about this?" she asked her father.

Her father appraised her with the lopsided smile he had, the relic of the block of ice to his face. "You can't fight your way through this," he said. His good ear and the ruin of his bad ear went back.

Kyla's own ears fell.

"I know," he said ruefully. "If you wanted a traditional marriage, you should have married another gnoll. This is what you get for marrying a human."

"Dad…"

"My hands are tied. The alliance between our family and the Ellsworth family puts both of us in a better position."

"Does that really matter to you?"

His ears went up and he chuckled. "No, but your mother and I want you to be happy." He set his mug of mead down and reached out to take Kyla's hand. "Our future in-laws are not the kind of people you can tussle in the mud with over a bone, and you are lucky they want to marry their surviving son out to a non-human to keep their lineage clean. It is best for both of you to go through the hoops they give you."

She shook her mane out. "I know, but even Mom is treating me like I'm still a cub to be told what to do, and not a proud fighter like you. I've grown and reached my full strength."

"That is because this doesn't just include us. Do you desire to lead a warband into battle and fall like the older Ellsworth boy, or do you wish to be comfortable and happy?"

She understood the question, but she dreamed sometimes of the glory she could earn in battle. "Can't you have both happiness and honor?"

Her father chuckled. "You would need a war for that, and wars have a way of getting out of control and destroying everything." He reached out to take her face gently. "Maybe someday you'll earn the right to wear the iron clasp of a veteran fighter in your mane, but never rush toward a war. The Ellsworth family got into that stupid squabble over farmland in the valley country to expand their holdings, and now they're a house in crisis. They need protection from their enemies, and we offer it. I would not let you marry the human boy if I thought it was dangerous for us. I also know not to interfere with the stirrings of your heart."

She sighed. "I guess, but what if they do decide to do something stupid? Does the marriage mean I would be able to fight and defend our holdings?"

"My fierce little cub, you have my passions, and I understand the hotness in your blood. I wear that hot temper every day on my face as a reminder of my youth and to warn me whenever I look at myself in the mirror in the morning of the dangers of such adventurism. Do not worry about a war. Layton Ellsworth is a good fifteen seasons older than me. He has a good many years left, but his appetite for foolish squabbles seems to be curbed. He grieves for a son lost and a legacy shaken. Even if he tries to do something, I will not willingly put us in a bind we can't meet muzzle first. By the time I'm too old to protect us, it will be Kane Ellsworth's time to lead his family."

She pointed her muzzle down. "I'm sorry if I've made things hard."

Her father shook his head. "It will all be fine, and I'm sure Canice can spin something out of this arrangement. Your mother is a persuasive woman and has the keenest ears for coin of anyone I know. You should enjoy your time before the wedding because it will be a long day."

୭

Her father's words were prophetic, for as the day of the ceremony drew near, more and more things came up that required Kyla's attention. There was a parade of courtiers and servants, both human and gnoll, that she had to give her claw up or claw down to about the tasks they were handling. Seating had to be arranged, meals had to be prepared, and it seemed the entire process took forever. She saw Kane only briefly, but he had his own preparations to be involved with. A few days before the wedding, she got to see him for an hour alone. She had remarked to him how she wanted to just leave and get married in a simple ceremony at a temple to whichever god was willing to bless them and be done with it. He agreed readily with the idea, but there was little they could do. Theirs was a political marriage, and while they were in love, there was great show and pomp required.

There was one thing Kyla had complete control over: her bridesmaids. Her mother had wanted to suggest some, but she'd insisted on two and only two: her friends Shara and Sibesli. It was their job to keep Kyla from pulling her fur out.

"How many ribbons are you going to have to tie into her mane?" Sibesli asked, as they sat in a tent set up in the sacred grove a few hours before the wedding.

"Enough that she's presentable," remarked Shara, as she carefully tied another knot of fabric into Kyla's mane.

"Too many," grumbled the bride. The tent had been furnished with elegant furniture, all carefully prepared for the bridal party. Plush chairs made the space comfortable, and a low brazier provided light and a little warmth. A dressing table sat with an array of brushes, while a rack held the wedding dress. Kyla had turned the low chair she sat on away from the dress so she didn't have to think about wearing that restrictive thing. Having to avoid tripping over a train was not something she was looking forward to. The loose, ankle length dress she wore with its multiple petticoats was annoying enough to her. She wanted to go with a simple hip wrap while she waited, but her mother had insisted something more formal, in case any of the servants had to come find her.

Sibesli shrugged. "I could braid it if you two'd let me. Maybe work a few silver beads in."

Shara glanced at the dwarf. "You say this, but I've seen your braid work. This is a job for a gnoll, and that's what needs to be done."

"Are you saying I'm not good enough to do this?" said Sibesli.

Kyla sighed. "Braids sound lovely, but Mom had clear instructions. The ribbons are supposed to be tied in neatly and orderly so I can be presentable in the eyes of the gods. She wasn't going to let me go with braids."

"And here I thought you were a fighter," said Sibesli.

Kyla shot her an icy look. "As if your marriage won't be similar."

"I'm a tradesperson, not a noble like you. There's not much resting on my marriage."

"Or mine," said Shara, as she carefully tied another ribbon in. "You're the noble."

The bride sighed. "We've only been landed for a few generations, and it's not a terribly gaudy home. You think I could just do something simple and be done with it, but no, everyone wants things. Everyone has specific requests and concerns that need to be met. It's driving me mad."

"Well, your station seems to have gone up with the marriage. Now you're a link between human and gnoll-kind. A way to the future of our peoples," said the other gnoll.

"Yes, but I don't want all that pressure," growled Kyla. "I just want to be me."

"You sound like your father," said Shara, "when your mother has once again roped him into another official court function he doesn't want to do."

"I guess," she mumbled as her friend tied on another ribbon.

"I think this is the last," she remarked. "What do you think, Sibesli?"

The dwarf got up and came around. "It looks good. A little wild, but that's what you wanted, yes?"

"Yeah. I wanted something that was formal yet still flowed."

"Kane won't care," grumbled Kyla.

"I know, but the ceremony isn't for him, or you. It's for the people around you," said the dwarf. "He sent you something via way of me to let you know that," she added, pulling out a brown glass bottle from a large embroidered bag she had brought with her.

Kyla took the bottle and sniffed at the top, her ears perking. She pulled the cork and took another sniff. "Plum brandy?"

"He told me you'd want a nip to steel your nerves."

Kyla's ears went down, and her head lowered. "He knows me too well."

"Oh, you should have told me," said Shara. "I also brought a bottle of grain spirits."

"Ha!" said Sibesli, and produced a second bottle from the bag. "We both know you. Dwarven style whisky, aged forty years deep in a mountain vault."

"My friends," said Kyla with a toothy grin. "We have a toast to make, but let's start with the elven wine I had them include in the tent."

Sibesli smiled. "I'll make a dwarf out of you yet."

℘

The elven wine was good, the brandy was excellent, but the dwarven whisky was when things started to get out of control. They had passed it around, and while Sibesli might have had her head on for the most part, the two gnolls did not.

"You know, we should have just gotten married already," said Kyla with a goofy grin. "All this waiting is boring."

"There's another hour till sunset I think," said Shara, reaching for the bottle and fumbling, trying to get it from Kyla.

"We should stop," said the dwarf with a belch. "You need to be able to stand."

"Ha! I can stand," remarked Kyla, staggering to her feet.

"Yes, but you're swaying."

Kyla stepped a few times and stopped. "So I am."

"As much as it pains me to say this, and it goes against my dwarven ancestors," said Sibesli, "but we need to put the bottle down."

Shara stood up. "There's a cleric here to do the ceremony. Maybe they can fix us up something," she said, trying to stumble toward the tent's entrance, and immediately tripping over the trunk that held spare clothes. Shara went down and there was a rip of fabric.

"Oh shit," said Kyla coming over. "Are you hurt?"

"Just my ego," said the other gnoll. "And maybe this dress."

Kyla squinted. "That's not the one for the ceremony, is it?"

"No, no. I haven't pulled that out yet, but we should change soon."

"Let me see what the cleric can do," said the dwarf, walking toward the entrance. "Hopefully they can whip up a quick tincture that cures hangovers."

"Does that use alcohol to make?" asked Kyla.

The dwarf shrugged. "It's that or you need to know a bit of magic or whatever to create it. I don't know. You've got to be sober enough to stand."

"I'm fine," declared the bride.

"No you're not."

"Okay, okay," said Kyla, walking back to where she had been sitting. "But if the cleric needs something for the tincture, this might help," she said, picking up the unopened bottle Shara had brought and handing it to the dwarf.

"Good plan. It's a good base I think," said Sibesli.

"Hey, hey, don't turn that into medicine now," said Shara getting up, trying to snatch the bottle back from the dwarf.

"We need to be presentable!" said the dwarf.

"That's my gift to Kyla though," she said, trying to get her claws on the bottle. Sibesli stepped back, but Shara managed to connect with the bottle and knock it out of her hands. It sailed through the air and straight into the fire.

They all froze. The bottle shattered, and there was a whooshing sound as the fire flashed and shot up toward the roof of the tent.

That set everyone in motion. Shara screamed as the fire singed her fur, and everyone jumped back. Black smoke poured from the fire as it expanded.

"Everyone out, now!" said the dwarf, and the three fled the tent quickly, running out into the grove set up for the bridal party.

Realizing they'd now set the tent on fire along with her wedding dress, Kyla felt a tightness grip her chest. Her mother was going to kill her, the Ellsworths were going to keep her from marrying Kane, and everything they'd all spent months planning was now ruined. She couldn't face that.

She glanced back at the black smoke pouring out from the top of the tent and made a snap decision. With her head swimming from the alcohol and now having destroyed her family name by trying to drink her friends under the table, the bride turned and plunged straight into the woods and disappeared into the trees.

Sibesli and Shara called out Kyla's name, but she was gone. The dwarf swore, took one look at the blazing fire still contained in the brazier, and turned to Shara.

"We need to go after her," said Sibesli.

"No," said Shara. "We should get Kane. There's only one person she's going to listen to right now."

They looked back at the tent. The smoke hole at the top was singed and blackened, but it hadn't caught. Instead, the fire was starting to settle back down. The wedding could still proceed as planned, but it would need its bride.

❧

The sacred grove of Hannaril was located in a large forest that some say dates to the age of the Old Gods. Massive trees of oak and ash were interspersed with ancient stands of yew. The forest was tended by elven druids, and generations of them had carefully nurtured it. Ancient trees grew tall and blocked out the sky, while a layer of dead leaves nurtured their twisting roots.

Kyla ran through the forest, not thinking of what to do, but just to get away. She tripped over roots and scrambled across fallen tree trunks to put distance behind her. Now, in the gathering gloom, her dress torn from branches and brambles she'd run past, she was out of stamina for running. Her footpaws aching from where rocks had cut at them, she was beginning to regret her decision. Her mother would be furious. Destroying the tent would be one thing, but leaving? Oh no, she'd have words with her daughter and there would be fangs in her face. Lots of angry fangs, and that was before she got to her father, who would also be disappointed.

Kane though, he'd understand, or at least she hoped he would. He was going through his own issues, marrying outside of his species. His parents didn't really approve of her, but she served a purpose, and if that's how they thought of her, it at least let them be together.

She sighed and slumped down against a tree. She had a pounding headache from all the wine and brandy she'd drank. Coming out here had made more sense when she'd been buzzed, but now she just felt like shit. She'd thrown up once already and she was lost. The wedding was ruined, the engagement was in danger, and here she was out in the woods with a torn dress, no lantern, and no weapon. All she had was her fangs and her nose, and that was not going to fix anything for her. Kyla was a disgrace.

She sobbed. Worse, she'd left him at the altar. If there was one thing that made this entire orchestrated dance tolerable, it was Kane, and even he would have good reason to be mad at her. She should go back, but could she really face everyone? She'd ruined everything her mother had worked to achieve, and now she was an outcast. All she could do was sit there and cry, tail tucked, ears down, not thinking, not moving, until she heard her name in the distance.

"Kyla…"

She cocked her head. Had they found her? What was she going to say? She was sorry for running away and burning down the tent? She stood up uncertainly, and looked to see which direction they were coming from, but night had fallen now. The forest was completely dark.

"Kyla…" called out a distant voice.

She swiveled her ears, trying to figure out where it was coming from and who it was.

"Kyla Tangledmane…" said the voice again, the words drifting strangely through the air. This wasn't a voice she recognized, yet it spoke with familiarity, as if the speaker knew her.

"Who's there?" she called out. There was no answer, but in the distance through the trees, there was a light she hadn't seen before. Cautiously, she headed toward the light, which flitted through the trees, casting a blue glow that seemed to be carried by someone moving jerkily.

"Who are you," she called out, trying to catch the light, stumbling through the trees in the dark.

"Come," said the voice with increasing urgency. "Come…"

Kyla broke into a sprint. Who was this? What did they want with her?

She was gaining on the light, and when it next ducked around a tree, she saw it clearly. There wasn't someone carrying a light there. Instead, it was a will-o'-wisp, one of the spirits of the forest itself, that was leading her on.

She slowed down then, her senses coming to her. Following a will-o'-wisp was dangerous. They were known to play tricks and one could easily lead you to your death if it wanted.

The blue light continued on and then disappeared from her vision. She crept forward cautiously. The will-o'-wisp had entered a clearing and it wasn't the only source of light there. Slowly she moved ahead, trying to be silent, but her footpaws crunched on the leaf litter. She stubbed a claw into a fallen branch, and that made her curse loudly.

"Come…" said the voice, clearer now. "Your destiny awaits you, Kyla Tangledmane."

She took a deep breath and squared her shoulders. Whoever this was knew who she was, so she walked forward toward the clearing.

The clearing was small and circular, and it was lit with candlelight. In the back sat a standing stone etched with runes covered in moss and worn down by time. Before it sat the oldest gnoll Kyla had ever seen. His fur was gray and the stripes in his pelt had faded. He was thin and boney as if he had not eaten in weeks, and yet the gaze from his one good eye was a piercing ember of coal that reflected the candlelight. The other was lost, a jagged scar across the face, the eye socket empty.

Near him was a brazier with herbs burning, and candles had been placed around the clearing. The will-o'-wisp was behind him, bobbing slowly around the standing stone. In front of him lay a cloth, covering something up.

"Come," he said, with a wispy voice that seemed to echo strangely in her head. "Let me show you your destiny."

"I know my destiny," Kyla said cautiously, still standing at the tree line. Maybe she was dreaming and had passed out.

The old gnoll regarded her coolly. "You know one of your destinies. I know inside of you your blood is hot, and you hunger for more. Now sit!" he commanded, as if he was speaking to a child.

She wanted to turn around, but something about the strange gnoll suggested he had great power. Carefully, she walked over like an obedient cub and sat down. The smoke from the burning herbs made her head hurt, and combined with the feeling of the alcohol, she winced in the light.

"You wish to answer the ancient call of Uratu, the hunter, and to fight. You long so much to be the great warrior you always were," said the seer. "You hunger for battle."

"It is true," she murmured.

"I know it is. Look into my eye, and see," he ordered.

A sober Kyla might have thought this was a bad idea, and yet in her state of intoxication, with the herbs tugging at her mind, she did so willingly. She looked straight into the seer's eye and she saw herself, proud and strong.

"You could be a great warrior," said the seer.

Her heart ached for what she saw. "I know, but my fate is not this."

"Your fate is yours!" said the seer, and then she saw herself charging into battle, a flail in one paw, a shield in the other, as nameless enemies fell before her. Other gnolls followed her into the fray. She was everything she wanted to be, and there was a surge of pride in herself. She could feel the heft of the weapon in her paws, and suddenly everything she worried about fell away.

"Do you see?" he asked.

"Yes," she whispered, entranced by the vision.

"Do you feel the hunger for battle within you?" he whispered to her. He was right in front of her, but he seemed so far away.

She hadn't felt it before, but now that she could see her fate, she felt the call to battle within her more clearly than she ever had. There was a hunger for it inside of her now that she had never felt before. She'd wanted to make her father proud, but now, she wanted to fight, not for just the glory, but because she could fight. She would be a great warrior like she dreamed about. "I do," she whispered.

"Then become what you are meant to be," he ordered and he blinked, breaking off the vision and contact. The old gnoll reached down and pulled back the cloth covering the item before him. It was a flail with a spiked ball on the end of a chain.

"Take this, and slay the first human you see with it, and you will know glory. Rivers of blood will flow before you, and your name will strike fear in those weak of heart. Many will submit to your will. War will be your shadow."

She wanted what he was offering so badly, yet she hesitated for a moment. Something was tugging at her consciousness. She looked up at the old gnoll with the one bright eye and unnaturally thin frame. He looked ravenous. "And if I don't?"

"You will be nothing more than a token on the arm of a man, never able to find the call to battle you long for. You will grow weak and die."

She would die? She didn't want that. Instinctively she reached for the weapon and clasped her paw around the handle. The leather wrapping the wood was warm and felt good in her paw. She hefted the flail, and the chains made a satisfying clatter. This was a brutal weapon, a dangerous weapon, but it would serve her well if she gave it what it wanted, and it wanted blood. She knew that once she held it.

"Good," said the seer. "Swear to me this vow. You will kill the first human you see and claim your birthright."

Kyla Tangledmane stood up, her blood hot and body hungry to fight, and she smiled with fangs. "I will kill the first human I see," she said, drunk on the herbs, an unnatural hunger coursing through her.

"Excellent, serve me well cub, and you will feed your hunger for war."

She turned to leave, and stepped toward the tree line, but she paused, curious what else he could tell her. Who were the troops she would lead? Who would she fight to bring glory to herself? She wanted very much to earn the iron clasp for her mane.

No, she didn't want the iron clasp. She needed it now. She hungered for it!

She looked back toward the seer, but he was gone. Where moments ago there had been candles there was now only ash and a bit of spilt wax. Only the will-o'-wisp was still there, and it wandered off into the forest.

꙳

Back in among the trees, she stalked through the woods, looking for the one the seer told her to kill. She would slaughter them as he told her to and then she would tell her mother she was not going to be part of her political games, but a leader of a warband. She'd take Kane with her, and she'd lead troops to glory.

Wait, Kane wasn't in her vision. She'd been leading only gnolls. Maybe he'd stay back in the camp of whomever she worked for.

She paused and put her free paw to her head, feeling the hunger for battle inside herself. Who was she fighting anyway? She tried to focus back on the vision, back on what she'd seen, but the headache made it hard to think clearly. She growled, annoyed with herself. It had been a village. There were people. Humans, dwarves, elves…

They weren't armed.

"Kyla! Kyla! Where are you!"

Her ears snapped back. Her prey was near. She screamed a reply with a voice hoarse and hungry. "Kane!"

"Kyla!" he yelled, and he came crashing through the woods toward the sound of her voice.

She wanted to run to him, wanted to wrap her arms around him, but she had the flail still in her paw, and she knew it would be easier to swing and hit him if he came to her, just as the seer wanted, so she waited for him. She would feed her hunger for battle soon.

Less than a minute later he broke through the trees, and he saw her when the light of the lantern he carried fell upon her. "Kyla," he said, coming up breathlessly. Kane Ellsworth practically threw himself against her, wrapping his free arm around her. She was a good bit taller than him, and his head easily fit under her muzzle.

He was unarmed, she noted as he had approached. He wouldn't be able to resist her attack.

"Are you hurt?" he asked. "I was worried about you," he said, embracing her in a hug.

She felt the flail in her paw. She felt her blood hammering in her head. Kill the first human you see, the seer had said. If he could see her future, he knew which human that would be. He knew what her fate would be.

"Kane," she whispered and gently pushed him away, and slowly lifted the flail with a clank of the chain.

He looked at her confusedly, and then he saw the flail, cruel and wicked. "I should have known you wouldn't come out here unarmed. The elves warned me not to go by myself, but I couldn't leave you out here alone."

All she had to do was step back and swing. She'd become a killer. A butcher. She could see the faces in her vision. They weren't warriors facing her down in combat. They were scared villagers trying to protect their homes from marauders.

To protect their village from her.

She looked at Kane, and she could visualize the impact the flail would make. The feeling of it crushing in his skull would be satisfying. He would scream only once before he died. Afterward, she would be covered in his blood, and nothing she said or did after that would be her own doing.

She knew then she would be just an avatar for war. That was what the seer had shown her. Her own parents would hunt her down if she did this, and worst of all, she'd break her own heart.

The flail slipped from her paw. The chain clattered as it fell.

"Kyla?"

She looked down at her paws and they were shaking.

"Kyla?" he said again. "Are you okay?"

She took a deep breath, and it all came back to her, as if some force had been holding her back.

"I don't know. I think I messed up."

"It's okay. The tent didn't catch," he said, "but why did you run out here armed with a weapon? There's nothing you needed to prove to me."

"I didn't come out here armed," she said softly.

He frowned. "You found the flail out here?"

She turned to look behind her. Now that the flail wasn't in her paws anymore, she no longer felt so hungry. "I was given it by someone."

"Who?"

"I'm not sure. They are a spirit of some kind, I think. They offered it to me if I fulfilled a vow for them."

Kane was well versed in history and knew a little magic himself, but that caused his breath to catch. "What did they want?"

Her voice wavered. "For me to kill the first human I saw. He showed me a vision where I was a great warrior, but now I realize he showed me the vision of me as a murderer and savage killer, taking from those who had little and striking them down." She lowered her muzzle so she could rub a paw across her forehead. She hunched over. "Ugh, I can still see it, I can taste the smoke of burning houses."

Some men would have backed way, but then not all men can date and marry outside of their species. Kane was not one to back down.

"It's okay. You had the sense not to do that," he said, taking one of her paws in his hands. "I know you couldn't do something like that."

As Kyla looked down at him, she wasn't completely sure if another human had found her first that she wouldn't have killed them to fulfil the vow. Yet even with mind still clouded by the drink and influenced by the herbs, she had not instinctively swung at him. She had not chosen the path of senseless war.

"I'm so sorry I ran off," she said with a sniff.

He squeezed her paw gently. "It's okay. I know this has been a lot for you. It's the same for me. We're doing this together though."

She wrapped her arms around him then, and pulled him to herself, and let herself feel the tension and confusion that had been riding upon her. "I don't deserve you, and I could have…" her voice cracked.

"Kyla, it's okay. That you didn't is what matters."

What could she say? Nothing. She just wrapped herself around Kane and pulled him close and she cried, holding him in the dark, unsure what to do.

~

Kyla was still holding onto Kane when Shara and Sibesli found them.

"You run too fast," said Sibesli to Kane, holding up a lantern at them both. "I've got short legs you know!"

"I had to find her," said Kane.

"At least Shara has the decency to stay with me."

"It's okay," said Kyla. "I'm safe now."

"Now?" asked Sibesli.

Kane nodded. "It's okay."

Shara was looking at the flail where it lay discarded. "Where did you get this?" she said, kneeling down to inspect the weapon. She went to pick it up and pulled back, as if the handle radiated heat.

"An old gnoll gave it to me. He was some type of seer. He wanted me to kill the first human I met with it. He asked I swear a vow to him I would do that."

Shara inhaled deeply. "Was he thin?" she asked seriously.

Kyla took a moment to look at the worry on Shara's face before she responded. "Unnaturally so."

"You met the Starving God of Hate," she whispered.

No one spoke for a minute before Kyla whispered, "I've never heard of this god."

"Few have, and that is for a good reason. He has no name. He is just hunger for death. To feed him is to embrace evil. To do his will is to fall before the other gods. He tempts those he thinks he can bend to his will to feed his hate for all living things," said Shara.

Kyla felt her stomach boil and wanted to curl up into a ball.

"Where did you see him?"

"There was a clearing, and a will-o'-wisp led me to him."

"He can summon the spirits of the dead to do his bidding, but his powers over them are limited. Show me where you saw him."

"Shouldn't we go back," asked Sibesli, "and let the elves know?"

"The elves will understand. Canice Tangledmane will understand. Kane's parents, well I'll handle them," said Shara. "We need to find the clearing."

Kane spoke up. "Understand what?"

"That I will perform your wedding ceremony in this grove tonight and marry you in the traditional manner of the gnolls."

The other three didn't say anything else.

"Come, we go to the grove immediately," said Shara.

"Is this wise?" asked Sibesli. "Getting married in a corrupted grove seems a bit unwise."

"Mother wanted an auspicious wedding, and I don't think this counts as auspicious."

Shara took a deep breath. "The Starving God of Hate lurks in darkness, looking to tempt those in distress to feed him. Rejecting him is the most favorable thing you can do, Kyla. To face your fear of his hate and declare your love in front of him as his spirit lurks in the darkness beyond? That is a powerful statement to the other gods of our people, and they will bless your union. Love is the thing the Starving God cannot stand the most. He has no power in the face of it."

Kyla looked at Kane. "Is that okay?"

Kane took a deep breath. "It's going to be a hard thing to convince my parents of."

"We do this first, and then we ask forgiveness," said Shara. "You can still do a ceremony before them, but I will fasten your hands together in the old way. I just need some of the ribbons from Kyla's mane and for Sibesli to witness."

"I can do that," said Sibesli. "What about the flail?"

Shara frowned at it. "That we'll leave to the elves to take care of. We must hurry."

Finding the clearing took over half an hour, but they were able to locate it. The grove was dark save for the two lanterns they had and the full moon. Shara bent down to examine the marks the candles had left and then leaned down to sniff at where the brazier had been. She wrinkled her nose.

"I'm not sure what herbs he burned, but it smells foul."

"It was intoxicating, whatever it was," said Kyla.

Sibesli and Kane in the meantime were inspecting the standing stone.

"This has been desecrated," said the dwarf. "Some of the protective runes have been scratched off."

Kane traced his hand over them. "Yes, but it could be restored," he said. "Time has worn this down. The name for whoever was buried here has been lost."

"Which makes it all the more important we do this, now," said Shara, standing up. "Kyla, turn around, and let me take some of the ribbon from your mane."

She obeyed and Shara carefully untied three ribbons, which she fastened together into a makeshift rope. Satisfied that her knots would hold, she had the two of them stand before the standing stone while placing the two lanterns on either side.

"Ready?" she asked them.

They nodded. Sibesli stood off to the side. Kyla and Kane grasped one paw to one hand.

"Tonight, here in this circle, I will wed you before the gods of gnolls, humans, and any others that will bear witness!" intoned Shara.

The wind picked up suddenly, a breeze blowing through the clearing. They could feel powers far greater themselves watching.

"Kyla Tangledmane, daughter of Canice Tangledmane, do you take Kane Ellsworth, son of Layton Ellsworth, into your pack to be your mate?" asked Shara.

"Kyla…" called the voice of the seer as the wind suddenly howled in protest. In that moment, she could almost feel the flail in her hand again, and again she saw the warrior she could be, if she would just kill the human and the dwarf. The Starving God would be pleased, and why wouldn't she want to make him happy?

"Kyla Tangledmane!" yelled Shara, firmly, breaking off the vision. "Do you take Kane as your mate?"

Kyla looked at Kane as the wind blew through the clearing and nodded. "Yes!"

"Kane Ellsworth, do you take Kyla Tangledmane as your mate, and will you join her pack, to love her as your wife, and to stand with her clan in war and in peace so that justice is served, even when there are no bones to crack and no meat to be had?"

"I do," he said.

Shara pulled out the ribbon. "Then I shall bind you paw to hand in matrimony," said the gnoll, stepping forward to tie Kyla's right handpaw to Kane's left hand. When it was done she turned to Sibesli.

"Sibesli Ironfell, as witness to this ceremony, and before any gods that choose to watch, do you swear the knot I have tied between these two in good cloth to be satisfactory?"

"I do," said Sibesli.

"Then in the old ways, before our gods, I declare you married and mated."

They kissed then, and in that moment Kyla knew she had made the right decision. The wind died down as the moon shone and Tholla, steward of the night, smiled down upon them. The lies of the Starving God of Hate were shown to be nothing more than lies, for his presence had fled the ceremony, unable to stand in the presence of their love.

Together the group returned to find the rest of the wedding party and to announce that the union had been made in defiance of the Starving God of Hate. The Ellsworth family was ready to declare war then in an uproar about this trickery, but the cleric who was to marry them stepped forward and bowed to Kyla and Kane. He declared their union the most blessed he'd ever seen and said that the gods would favor them both. The complaints on the lips of the Ellsworth family died then, and a feast was declared for all present.

And the best part of that night for Kyla? She never wore that wedding dress with its ornate lace and dark red fabric she felt clashed with her pelt.

Acknowledgements

I didn't start writing this book planning to write a book, I was just writing myths for my character Ingot to know. However, Patreon gave me a place to put them, and I am immensely grateful for everyone who pledged over the years. Without my patrons on Patreon, this book would never have happened. I simply never would have written as many stories as I did.

I need to thank Utunu who provided the genesis for where the first bits of these stories came from, and who always pushed me to make these stories more gnollish. I would also like to thank the other two members of my writing group, Slip-Wolf and Domus Vocis, for reading all of these tales and providing valuable feedback. I'd also like to thank the friends I've had a chance to play Dungeons & Dragons and other RPGs with over the years for all the fun times that helped inspire me to write these tales. I'd also like to thank the players of the first campaign I ever managed to finish as a dungeon master for seventy-one sessions of fun. Thank you to Scribbles, Fugue, Atrix, and Utunu for playing through the entire thing with me, thank you to TJ Minde, Kiri, and Ocean

Tigrox for playing when you could, and thank you to Kayodé for jumping in late and rolling with the insanity. Everyone I've played an RPG with has helped me think about lore in a way that let me shape this book, both with how you played your characters and the questions you asked me when I've run games.

Finally, I'd like to thank my fiancé Othello for supporting me through another book, and for his interest in different kinds of storytelling. Without him, I wouldn't be able to finish a book.

About the Author

NightEyes DaySpring is a known troublemaker who is rumored to have a penchant for coffee and an interest in dead, ancient civilizations. He has been writing furry fiction for over twenty years, and over thirty-five of his short stories have been published. His work has appeared in various anthologies, including *Werewolves vs. Fascism*, *Heat*, and *FANG*. He also has contributed multiple stories to *The Voice of Dog* podcast, and he recently published his first novel, *Scars of the Golden Dancer*. Currently, NightEyes resides in Florida with his fiancé, where in his spare time he masquerades as an IT professional, plays board games, and doodles.

Visit his website, *nighteyes-dayspring.com*, for more about his writing, or find out where he is on social media at *nighteyes.carrd.co*.

About the Artist

Fruitz is a fox and an illustrator who is sometimes also an editor and designer. He started off drawing comics but is now experimenting with more painterly art styles. He loves Chicago with all his heart.

You can find him on Twitter (@FruitzJam) causing chaos.